VAMPIRE GAMES

////

J.R. RAIN

THE VAMPIRE FOR HIRE SERIES

Published by
Crop Circle Books
212 Third Crater, Moon

Printed in the United States of America.

ISBN-13: 978-1548119409
ISBN-10: 1548119407

Dedication

To those who care for the animals of this world.

Acknowledgments

A special thank you to Eve Paludan, Sandy Johnston, Elaine Babich and P.J. Day.

"And what is a vampire? It is something the creeps but never crawls. It is something that drinks but never feasts. It is something unseen but never forgotten." —*Diary of the Undead*

"There, on our favorite seat, the silver light of the moon struck a half-reclining figure, snowy white...something dark stood behind the seat where the white figure shone, and bent over it. What it was, whether man or beast, I could not tell." — *Dracula*

1.

Judge Judy was letting this online con artist know what a scumbag he was—and I was loving every minute of it—when my doorbell rang. I nearly ignored it. Nearly. I mean, she was so very close to having this guy in tears.

Except I knew this was a client at the door. And clients paid the bills.

I reluctantly clicked off the show, set aside the Windex bottle and rag I had forgotten I was holding, and headed for the front door. As I did so, I instinctively reached up for the pair of Oakley wraparound sunglasses that were no longer there. My next conditioned movement was to check my arms and face and hands for sunscreen—which wasn't there, either.

Wasn't there, and wasn't needed.

That is, not since I'd donned the emerald medallion two weeks ago. A medallion that had literally changed my life. A medallion that, curiously, no longer existed.

Two weeks ago, shortly after watching my first sunrise in seven years, I had reached down for the medallion, only to discover it was missing. Left behind had been a disc-shaped burn in my skin and the empty leather strap that had been holding the medallion.

Fang had thought my body *absorbed* the medallion. I had thought that sounded crazy as hell. Fang had reminded me that a skin-absorbing medallion was actually one of the least-craziest things to happen to me in seven years.

Now, two weeks later, there still remained a faint outline of the medallion on my upper chest, seared into my skin.

I'm such a weirdo, I thought, and settled for reaching up and checking on my hair. Since mirrors were still out of the question, I had become a master at feeling my way through a good hair day. At least, I hoped they were good hair days.

As I stood before the front door, a lingering trepidation remained. After all, sunlight had been my enemy for so many years.

You can do this, I thought.

And I did. I opened the front door wide as sunlight splashed in. Brilliant sunlight. Splashing over me, but my skin felt...nothing. I felt nothing, and that was the greatest feeling of all.

No searing pain. No gasping sounds. No stumbling around and covering my eyes. No shrinking like a monster from the light of the day.

Such a weirdo.

Maybe. But now, not so weird.

Thank God.

Today, I was wearing torn jeans and a cute blouse, a sleeveless blouse, no less. Most importantly, I wasn't wearing multiple layers of clothing or one of my epic sunhats. Or satellite dishes, as a client had once called them.

It was just me. And that felt good. Damned good.

The man standing in the doorway was smaller than I expected. He was wearing a Chicago Bulls tank top and basketball shorts and high-top sneakers. He looked like he might have just stepped off the courts or raided a Foot Locker. The detailed tattoos that ran up and down his arms—and even along his neck—seemed to tell a story about something, although I couldn't puzzle it out at first blush.

"Russell?" I said.

"That's me," he said softly. "You must be Ms. Moon."

He dipped his head in a way that I found adorable. The dip was part greeting, part submission, and partly to let me know that he came in peace. We shook hands and I led him to my office in the back of my house, passing Anthony's empty room along the way. Well, not entirely empty. A pair of his white briefs sat in the middle of the floor, briefs that had seen better—and whiter—days. I reached in and quickly shut the door before my client got a good look at the mother of all skid marks.

Superman had Lex Luthor. Batman had the Joker. I had Anthony's skid marks.

Once safe in my office, I showed Russell to one of my client chairs and took a seat behind my cluttered desk.

"So, what can I do for you, Russell?" I asked.

"Jacky says you might be able to help me."

"Jacky, the boxing trainer?"

"Yes," he said.

"Jacky say anything else?"

"Only that you are a freak of nature."

I grinned. "He's always thought highly of me. What kind of help do you need?"

He looked at me. Straight in the eye. He held my gaze for a heartbeat or two, then said, "Somebody died accidentally...except I don't think it was an accident."

I nodded and did a quick psychic scan of the young man sitting before me. I sensed a heavy heart. Pain. Confusion. I sensed a lot of things. Most important, I did not sense that he was a killer.

"Tell me about it," I said.

2.

Russell Baker was a boxer.

A damn good one, too, apparently. He was twenty-five, fought in the coveted welterweight division, had a record of 22-3, and was moving quickly up the rankings. There were whispers that he might fight Manny Pacquiao—or Floyd Mayweather, Jr. His management was presently negotiating a fight on HBO. He'd already fought around the world: Tokyo, Dubai, South Africa. He'd already beaten some of the top contenders in the world. Only the best remained. Only the champions remained. Russell Baker was on top of the boxing world and nothing could slow him down.

That was, until his last fight.

When he had killed a man in the ring.

Russell paused in his narrative, and I waited. He was a good-looking guy, clearly roped with muscle under his thin tee-shirt. His nose was wide and flat, which I suspected was perfect for boxing. A long, pointed nose probably got broken routinely. He was also small, perhaps just a few inches taller than me. Welterweights must be the little guys. If I had to guess, I would have said that he was exactly half the size of Kingsley.

After collecting himself, Russell continued. The fight had been last month, in Vegas. Russell had been working his way through the top ten fighters in his weight class. According to Russell, rankings were influenced by a boxer's win-loss record, the difficulty of one's opponents, and how convincing one's victories were. The ultimate goal was to challenge for a title.

Last month, he'd fought the #7 ranked contender. Russell himself had currently been ranked #8. The fight was aired live on ESPN. The crowd had been full of celebrities. Up through three rounds, it had been a routine-enough fight, with Russell feeling confident and strong.

That is, until the fourth round.

It had been a short, straight punch to the side of the face. A hard punch. One that, if landed squarely, would rock most opponents. And Russell had landed it squarely. His opponent's head snapped back nicely. Russell had moved in closer to land another punch, but his opponent, Caesar Marquez, was already on his way to the mat.

Russell had been confused. The punch had been solid, sure, but not a knockout punch. But there was Caesar Marquez, out cold, motionless. Russell had celebrated, but not for long, not when Caesar remained motionless and a crowd began swarming around his fallen opponent.

Russell stopped talking and looked away, tears in his eyes. He unconsciously rubbed his knuckles, which were, I noticed, puffy and scarred. An IM message box appeared on the computer screen before me. It was Fang.

You there, Moon Dance?

I leaned forward and tapped a few keys: *I am, but working. Talk soon, okay?*

The butler did it, Moon Dance. Always the butler.

I shook my head and closed the box. Admittedly, I was mildly surprised that the box appeared. Fang always seemed to know when I was working—and respected my time with my clients. I frowned at that as I turned my attention back to Russell.

"May I ask how your opponent died?" I asked, lowering my voice.

"That's a good question, Ms. Moon."

"Please call me Sam."

He nodded. "Officially, they called it brain damage. Unofficially, they found nothing."

"How do you know this?"

"The M.E. told me. He personally called me up and told me that he couldn't find anything other than some bleeding—enough to officially label it a brain hemorrhage, but not enough to cause death. At least, not in the opinion of the medical examiner."

"Yes."

"So, why are you here, Russ?" I asked, trying out a nickname to get him to spill more details.

He continued rubbing his knuckles. His foot, which was crossed over his knee, was jiggling and shaking. Now he rubbed the back of his neck. The bicep that bulged as he did so was...interesting.

"I don't know, Sam. I don't know why I'm here."

"Yes, you do," I said. "Why are you here, Russell?"

"Because I don't think I killed him."

"If you didn't kill him, then who—or what—did?"

"I don't know, Sam. I guess that's why I'm here. I want you to help me find out how he died."

I sat back and folded my hands over my flattish stomach. Flat enough for me, anyway. I sensed so many emotions coming from Russ that it was hard to get a handle on them. Sensing emotion and reading minds are two different things. I wasn't close enough to Russ to read his mind, but his emotions were fair game to anyone sensitive enough to understand them.

Mostly, I sensed guilt coming off him. Wave after wave of it. I sensed that Russell hadn't been able to move forward from this fight and had been unable to deal with what had happened last month.

He needed answers. Real answers. Not the suspicious whisperings of a medical examiner.

"And what if I discover that you really did kill him, Russell?" I asked.

"Then I can live with that, but I need to know," he said, wiping his eyes and looking away. "I need to know for sure."

"Knowing is good," I said.

"Knowing is everything," he said, and I didn't doubt it for a second.

I nodded. "I'll need names and contact info."

He said he would email me everything I needed. We next discussed my retainer fee and, once done, he handed over his credit card. I spent the next few minutes embarrassing myself until I finally figured out how to use my iPhone credit card swiper. If I could have turned red, I would have.

We next shook hands, and if he noticed my cold flesh, he didn't show it. Or was too polite to show it.

As he left my office, I couldn't help but notice the dark cloud that surrounded him. His aura.

Guilt, I knew, was eating him alive.

He needed answers.

Badly.

3.

When Russell had gone, I brought up Google and researched the hell out of him.

In particular, I found the fight in question. The fight with Caesar Marquez had been a big deal, apparently. Both fighters were considered front runners to eventually contend for the welterweight title. Both fighters were roughly the same age. Same height. Same records. Same everything.

Except, now one was dead.

And the other was living with punishing, crushing guilt. I knew this. I had felt it from Russell, coming off him in wave after wave.

The crushing guilt was the least of my concerns. The black halo that completely surrounded his body was a different matter. A very serious matter.

Perhaps it was not so serious to others, but to me, I knew the implications. Russell needed help. He also needed protection. And, considering the vast amount of guilt he was dealing with...perhaps he needed protection from himself.

No, he hadn't appeared suicidal, but I was also no expert in psychological issues. And since I wasn't close enough to him to read his thoughts, all I had to go on were my gut impressions.

And my gut told me that he had a very heavy heart.

Baker vs. Marquez hadn't been a big pay-per-view event, but HBO had hyped it up pretty good. All in all, the fight had lasted four rounds. Up through three rounds, two judges had scored the fight in favor of Russell, but one had it in favor of Caesar. Pretty even.

That is, until "the punch."

I wanted to see the punch for myself. It turned out that YouTube had some pretty grisly videos on their website. In fact, there were easily a half dozen such boxing death videos. I first watched Russell's fight, then forced myself to watch the other five, too, for comparison.

Most of the videos showed two guys hammering each other in the ring. Generally, one guy was doing a lot of hammering, and one guy was doing a lot of receiving. At least that was the trend. In five of the six fights, one opponent was clearly dominating the other opponent.

But not in Russell's fight.

Their fight, at least to my untrained eye—and the truth was, I was perhaps more trained than most —their fight seemed fairly even, as the judge's scorecards had indicated.

Both fighters were trading punches. Both fighters were backing away. Both fighters were circling. Russell jabbed. Marquez blocked. Marquez circled, Russell followed. Both had quick feet. Quick hands. No obvious blood. No one staggered like in the other five video clips. No one was obviously getting their brains beaten in.

And there it was.

The punch.

It was a short, straight punch, designed to be used when two opponents were close-in to each other. Not a lot of back swing. Just power the fist at about shoulder height and use your weight to drive the punch home. Jacky had taught it to me years ago, and it was a common punch to use when practicing with the heavy bag. Myself, I had probably delivered thousands of such punches. They weren't generally considered knockout punches, although, if delivered with enough force, could certainly stun an opponent.

Except Marquez didn't look stunned.

He looked dead.

Prior to the punch, they had both been fighting an inside game, heads ducked, juking, bobbing and weaving, each looking for an opening. Russell saw his and struck, cobra-fast.

Marquez's head snapped back.

HBO had been right there to capture the next image fairly close up. Marquez's eyes rolled up. I saw the whites of them clearly. His hands dropped to his sides.

Russell had been about to deliver another blow when he clearly saw that something wasn't right with his opponent.

As Marquez's hands went limp, so did his knees and legs, and now he was falling forward, landing hard on his chest and face, where he proceeded to lay, unmoving.

I saw that Russell's first instinct was to help him —and I admired him for that—but then his trainer bull-rushed him and lifted him up off his feet. And as his trainer ran him wildly around the ring, I saw Russell trying to look back to his fallen foe.

The longer Caesar Marquez lay unmoving, the more chaotic the ring became. People swarmed and buzzed around him. Russell fought to get close to him. A stretcher appeared through the crowd and soon Caesar was being threaded through the ropes, through the crowd, and down a side aisle into what I assumed were the locker rooms.

I stopped the video and studied the crowded ring. Dozens of faces. Some confused, some concerned, many excited. Men, mostly, but a few women.

I replayed the video again and again. Watching his trainers, watching the crowd, looking for anything that gave any indication that someone might have known what was about to go down.

But nothing stood out.
Nothing at all.

4.

"So, do you still need to sleep during the day?" Kingsley asked, or, at least, I think he asked. Words had a tendency to get muffled when spoken around a side of beef.

We were at Mulberry Street Ristorante in downtown Fullerton, sitting by the window, drinking wine and eating steak. Just like regular people.

Of course, one of us wasn't so much eating their steak, as slurping the bloody juice pooling around it, and the other wasn't so much eating his steak, as wolfing it down.

I nodded. "I'm still a creature of the night, if that's what you're asking. And, yes, I still need to sleep during the day. I'm still weak during the day. I still feel like crap when I have to get up and pick up the kids during the day. The medallion only gives me the ability to *tolerate* the sun."

"No more burning?" he asked between bites.

"No more burning."

Mulberry's was busy tonight. It was busy every night, as far as I could tell. It was our restaurant of choice, especially since the cooks and waiters here were used to my orders of raw meat, extra bloody.

Now, as I watched Kingsley tear through his meat in record time, something occurred to me. "Now I have a question for you."

"Shoot."

"Were you always this big?"

"Big…how?"

"Big, as in I've actually seen you turn sideways to go through doorways."

"Only some doors, and, no, the big part came later."

"How much later?"

"Over time. Decades. Little by little, after each transformation."

"You mean, you grew after each transformation?"

"Yes. At least, as far as I could tell."

"But why?" I asked.

"Survival, I think."

"But you're already immortal," I said, lowering my voice.

"A weak immortal doesn't get one very far,

Sam. And remember, I can't turn into—" and now he lowered his voice to a low growl— "the thing I turn into, on cue. That happens only once a month, and generally in a locked room. And when it does happen, I'm often out of my mind. Gone to the world for the whole night."

"While something else takes over your body."

"Right," he said.

"So, being big in your daily life has its benefits."

"Of course. Stronger, faster, able to protect myself."

"So how big were you before?"

"Big enough, but not this big."

"Do all werewolves get as big as you?"

"Some bigger."

I said, "I haven't gotten bigger. If anything, I've gotten smaller."

"And you won't get bigger because each night you're at full strength. And even during the day you're not completely incapacitated."

"No," I said. "Even though I feel weaker during the day, I'm still far stronger than I used to be."

I recalled my boxing match with the Marine last year, the match that had occurred just before sundown. Sure, I had felt like crap, but I was still strong enough to take down America's finest.

"Also," added Kingsley, reaching over and cutting off a chunk of my nearly raw steak, "it's just the nature of my kind."

"For the host to grow big," I said.

"Right. We all have our quirks."

"I think your quirks are better than my quirks," I said.

"And who among us can fly?" he asked.

I thought about that. "Good point."

As the waiter refilled our glasses of wine, Kingsley asked what I was working on these days. I told him about my latest case, and as I did so, Kingsley began nodding. Turns out he'd seen the fight live on HBO.

"Wasn't much of a punch," he said. "Not enough to kill a man."

"Or so we think," I said. After all, I had done some research on the subject. "We still don't know his condition prior to the fight, or the amount of punches he'd taken in practice and other fights."

Kingsley shrugged. "True. Either way, it wasn't much of a punch; in fact, I thought the fight was pretty even up to that point. What's your gut tell you?"

I shrugged too, but, unlike Kingsley, my shrug didn't look like two land masses heaving. I said, "Nothing yet, although I think Russell's grasping at straws."

Kingsley nodded. "Looking for a way to live with his guilt, perhaps."

"Perhaps," I said. "One thing is clear: It's eating him alive. Literally." I told Kingsley about the black halo I'd seen around the young boxer.

"The same halo you saw around your son?"

"The same."

"What's it mean?" asked Kingsley.
"It means he needs help. Lots of help."

5.

It was after hours and I was sitting in Jacky's office.

Jacky, if possible, looked even smaller than usual as he sat behind a dented metal desk. He was drinking an orange Gatorade which, I think, was the classic Gatorade. Of course, if I drank Gatorade now, I would heave it up in a glorious orange fountain.

Jacky, of course, didn't need to know that, and since I only spent a few hours a week with the guy —and most of that was spent with him yelling at me to keep my hands up—I hadn't yet developed a telepathic rapport with him.

Which was just as well. I seriously suspected that the old man had suffered some brain damage himself. He'd been a champion back in the day. And in Jacky's case, "back in the day" meant the early fifties in Ireland.

Jacky had spent the past few decades here in Fullerton. At one point his gym had been a happening place for up-and-coming boxers, with Jacky himself training a handful of champions. That is, until downtown Fullerton had become so trendy that Jacky—perhaps a better businessman than I'd given him credit for—had decided to turn his gym into a women's self-defense studio.

Then again, if I was a spunky old man, I'd rather train cute women, too.

Anyway, when Jacky finished off the Gatorade, he wiped the back of his hand across his mouth, dropped the empty bottle into a nearby wastebasket and sat back.

"What did you think of the kid?" he asked, speaking in an Irish accent so thick that you would think he was only now making his way through Ellis Island.

"I think the kid is deeply troubled," I said. "And I don't blame him."

Jacky nodded. He seemed uncomfortable in his office. He seemed less himself, somehow. Out there, in the gym, he was larger than life, even though he was only a few inches taller than me. In here, at day's end, he looked like a shell of himself. He looked tired. Old. But not weak. Never weak. Even in quiet repose, the man looked like he wanted to punch something.

"Russ isn't the first lad to kill somebody in the ring, and he won't be the last. And usually it plays with a fighter's head, so much so that they ain't ever much the same again."

"He feels guilt," I said.

"They all do. Except it's part of the risk we take. Each kid knows that his next fight might be his last."

"Then why did you send him to me?"

Jacky didn't answer immediately. Through his closed door, I could hear someone sweeping and whistling. A door slammed somewhere, and I heard two women giggling down a hallway that I knew led to the female locker rooms.

"It's part of the risk, yes, but something about this one doesn't smell right."

I waited. I wanted to hear it from Jacky, someone who had seen tens of thousands of punches thrown in his lifetime. Jacky rubbed his knuckles as he formulated his thoughts. I wondered how difficult it was for Jacky to formulate his thoughts. How much brain damage had the old Irishman suffered?

There had to be some. His aura, which was mostly light blue and ironically serene, appeared bright red around his head. The bright red, I knew, was the body fighting something, perhaps a disease. Or dealing with an injury.

The Irishman rubbed his face and seemed to have lost his train of thought. The reddish aura around his head flared briefly.

I said gently, "You were saying something about this fight not smelling right."

"Was I now?"

"Yes."

"Which fight?"

"Baker vs. Marquez."

He nodded and rubbed the back of his neck and gritted his teeth. "It's hell getting old, Sam."

"So I'm told."

"And this noggin of mine just ain't right sometimes."

"Mine either."

He nodded, but I wasn't sure he'd heard me. He said, "Routine fight. No one beating up no one. Judges had Baker up a few rounds, but the truth is, they were only just beginning to feel each other out. No one had taken control yet. It was even as hell."

"Were you there?" I asked.

"At the fight? Hell, no. The wife doesn't let me anywhere near Vegas these days. She's afraid I'll spend our retirement—and then I'll never get to leave this damn gym."

"You love this damn gym," I said.

He winked at me, and I saw that there were tears in his eyes. Where the tears came from and why, I didn't exactly know. "More than anything," he said.

"You watched the fight on TV?"

"Which fight?"

"Baker vs. Marquez."

"Yes, of course. Russ is a local boy. He trains here sometimes. I showed him my best moves, and he never forgot his roots. Got to love a kid like that."

"Yes."

"Damn shame what happened. He ain't no killer. They were just boxing. Trading jabs, the occasional straight shot or hook. Nothing landed yet. Nothing really. No reason a kid should be dead."

Jacky fell silent and absently wiped the tears from his eyes. His knuckles were crisscrossed with scar tissue. I imagined Jacky raising hell in the streets of Dublin.

"So, what are you saying, Jacky?"

"I'm saying, in one fell swoop, two top contenders have disappeared. One's dead, and the other might as well be dead. There's something to that, Sam, something worth looking into."

I nodded, thinking about that, as Jacky sat back and closed his eyes and rubbed the scar tissue along his knuckles.

6.

You there, Moon Dance?

The IM box appeared on my laptop screen as I was packing my bags in my room. I quickly tossed my unfolded sweater in my suitcase. It was only February. Even Vegas was cold in February.

To what do I owe the pleasure, Fang?

I need to talk to you.

In person?

Maybe. No. I don't know.

What's going on, Fang?

There was a pause, and I was suddenly alarmed to discover my normally dormant heart had picked up its pace. It thudded steadily against my ribs, rocking me slightly. Normally, my own beating heart went unnoticed, which wasn't too surprising since these days it generally only beat about five times a minute.

Something was wrong. Or something could *potentially* be wrong. Or something was just...*off*. For starters, Fang seemed unusually closed to me. Not to mention, he didn't seem to be picking up on my own increasingly worried thoughts. What the hell was going on?

The little pencil icon appeared in the IM box, which meant Fang was typing something. A moment later, his words appeared:

I recently...met someone.

Would this someone happen to be a female?

Yes.

This wasn't horrible news. At least, not for me. I liked Fang. I appreciated his friendship and help. But I had always felt he had an ulterior motive: he wanted something from me. And what he wanted, he had made clear a year ago.

He wanted me to *turn* him.

Although I didn't doubt that he loved me, I always wondered where the love originated. Was it for me, or for what I am? A thought suddenly occurred to me, and I voiced it. Or, rather, wrote it:

Is this woman a...vampire?

Yes.

A real vampire?

A real vampire, Moon Dance.

May I ask her name?

You know her.

Something inside me turned to ice, which, for me, is saying something. I exhaled a steady stream of cold air, and wrote: *Detective Rachel Hanner.*

Yes.

How did you two meet?

She came in the other night, sat at the bar. Ordered a glass of white wine, same as you.

I read his words and would have held my breath, except I was never sure when I held my breath these days. He went on:

There was something about her. Something...otherworldly. The way she stared at me. Her small, precise movements. Her faint accent. It wasn't long before I suspected what she was.

I waited, re-reading his words, thinking hard, puzzling through this. What did this mean? I didn't know yet.

It wasn't until later, after her second glass of wine, that I realized she had been reading my mind. Her intrusion wasn't obvious. Not like the way I know when you're in there. I mean, I can always feel when you're in my mind, Moon Dance. Touching down here and there.

He paused and I was truly feeling sick. Down the hallway, I heard Anthony snoring lightly. Music came from Tammy's room. The house was locked. I always kept it locked. What was Hanner up to? I didn't know, but I had that creepy-ass feeling of being watched. Of course, with me, it might be more than a feeling.

I stood and walked over to my main window and looked out into the cul-de-sac. No one was out there. At least, not that I could see. All the cars on the street I recognized. But with Hanner—the only other vampire that I knew personally—she could be anywhere. She could be sitting on my roof, for all I knew. I shivered.

Jesus, I thought.

I sat back down and Fang's next message appeared almost instantaneously: *I think within a few minutes, she knew all my secrets. All of them.*

I knew what Fang meant. The man had some killer secrets. Literally. The kind that would send him back to jail—or a mental institution—for the rest of his life.

I see, I wrote, mostly to let Fang know I was still here.

She showed me her badge and told me she knew who I was. She called me by my name...my real name. She next gave me her home address and told me to meet her there after work.

When was this?

Last night.

"Shit," I whispered.

What happened next, Fang?

I wondered if Fang knew what had happened. After all, I knew that Hanner had a...gift for removing memories. Indeed, I sensed a lot of vagueness from Fang, and it was clear that our personal connection had been broken, somehow. I thought Hanner had something to do with that.

I'm...I'm not really sure, he wrote, confirming my suspicions.

I had a vision of blood, a lot of blood. Fang might have been more closed off to me than normal and, although I wasn't sure what the hell was going on, we still seemed to have some sort of connection.

Enough for me to see the blood.

But most disturbing of all—

I wrote: *You drank blood.*

He paused only slightly before writing: *Yes, Moon Dance.*

I sensed his shame, but I also sensed his excitement. Fang had grown up with elongated canine teeth, a rare defect that had grown into an even rarer psychosis: as a youth, he began to actually believe he was a vampire. Crazy, but that was exactly what it was.

Crazy.

His psychosis had led to the death of his girlfriend, a teenage girl who had been partially bled to death...and partially consumed.

By Fang.

His escape from a high-security mental institution had been in all the papers, and his subsequent manhunt had been well documented. But he had slipped away.

And assumed a new identity.

Aaron Parker, aka Fang, now went by the official name of Eli Roberts—and how he landed in my life was one of coincidence and obsession.

Although I doubted he still saw himself as a real vampire, I knew he retained a hunger for blood. I knew this because every now and then I would see it in his thoughts. His hunger. But over the years, he had controlled himself. Controlled *it*.

We were both silent. Or, rather, the IM message box remained silent. I wasn't sure what to say. I sensed that Hanner was working her way into his world, but for what reason, I didn't know. But one thing I did know: none of it was good.

So, what will you do now, Fang? I finally wrote, deciding on the direct path. What else could I say?

I don't know, Moon Dance.

Did she threaten you?

She didn't have to. I understand the implications. I'm a fugitive. She's a cop. Things could go very badly for me.

Did she say what she wanted?

From me? Not yet.

She wants something from you, Fang.

I sensed him nodding, and after a moment, he wrote: *I know.*

But I sensed he was holding something back, and finally wrote: *There's something else, isn't there, Fang?*

Yes, Moon Dance.

I waited, suddenly afraid of the answer.

After a moment, he wrote: *She wants to give me something, Moon Dance. The one thing you wouldn't do for me, the one thing you wouldn't give me.*

Ah, Fang...
Yes, Moon Dance. Immortality.

7.

The flight to Vegas was of the commercial airline type.

Although only forty-five minutes from John Wayne Airport in Santa Ana, I had plenty of time to think about Fang and Hanner. How she had found him, I didn't know. I suspected she had followed me or had someone watch me. That she had gone over my phone records wasn't out of the realm of possibility, either. Generally, the police needed a damn good reason to scour one's phone records. She could have made up a reason, or done so secretly, in a way that I wasn't aware of. Private investigators don't have such access to phone records. A homicide investigator would.

The plane hit some turbulence, which I ignored.

Turbulence didn't bother me. Nor did the thought of the plane plummeting to Earth in a fireball. I was fairly certain I would have been the one passenger on board to walk away from such a crash. Or fly away.

If Hanner had gone the phone record route, she would have seen the pathetic few times that Danny had called to speak to his own children—and the pathetic short amount of time he had spent talking to them, as well.

She would have also seen the occasional phone call from Eli Roberts, aka Aaron Parker, aka Fang.

Some minor research into Eli's background would have netted a curious result: his background didn't go very far back. A quick scan of his current background would have resulted in seeing his current employment. From there, all she would have had to do was swing by for a visit...

And scan his thoughts.

She would have known then who he was. No secrets would have been hidden from her. She would have known his murderous past, and his current desires.

But why?

Hanner had proven to be helpful in the past, but perhaps she was just covering for her own kind. After all, she had, on more than one occasion, successfully hidden my supernatural activity from the local police. More than helping me, we had drunk blood together. Discussed our kids together. Laughed together. I had found her insightful and knowledgeable, if not a little feral. Whereas I fought to hold onto my humanity—at least what I thought made me human—Hanner clearly embraced her vampiric nature. She was all vampire, through and through, and any vestiges of humanness were long, long gone.

As an immortal, her thoughts were closed to me, so I could only guess what her intentions were. Clearly, she was obsessed with me. If not obsessed, then overly *aware*. Perhaps she was this way with all local vampires. Or with any vampires with whom she crossed paths. Perhaps she considered all other vampires her enemies.

I shook my head at that thought and leaned back in my economy seat. No, if she considered all vampires her enemies, then she wouldn't have supported a local blood dealer—the actor, Robert Mason—who, in turn, provided blood for many other vampires.

Perhaps her interest in me had something more to do with our last conversation, when she had said that I was a rare breed.

That I had special gifts.

That I could do things other vampires couldn't.

Or perhaps her interest in me had something to do with the old vampire who had turned me seven years ago. The old vampire, now dead thanks to Rand the Vampire Hunter. He, of the cute buns.

I thought about all of this as the plane landed. A jolting landing. I, myself, landed far smoother, of course. Which reminded me: According to Hanner,

I was one of the few vampires who could transform.

When the plane finally came to a stop, I stood with others, got my bags like the others, and waited in line to shuffle off the plane. Like the others.

But I was not like the others.

No, I was not like them at all.

8.

Dr. Herbert Sculler looked like a character out of a Tim Burton movie.

The short doctor wore round glasses and a lab coat that looked far too big for him. His face was whiter than my own and he smiled far too often, at least too often for a medical examiner who spent his days around corpses.

We were sitting in his office, which was next to his examining room. There was a man lying on one of the tables, under a sheet, waiting patiently for the doctor's return.

Sculler's office was small. I suspected it was so because he spent the majority of his time in the examining room. There, against the far wall, one, two, three corpses were lined up in plastic bags on shelves.

More interesting was the male spirit standing off to the side of the dead man in the examining room. The spirit crackled with energy, even when standing motionless. So far, it had not taken its eyes off the body under the blanket. From here, I could see two dark holes in the spirit's chest, which I knew to be bullet wounds. After many months of seeing the dead, I knew that spirits often mirrored their appearance at death.

Welcome to my life.

The spirit merely stood there and stared, wavering in and out of existence. Meaning one moment he was a fairly full-formed human-shape; the next, he was nothing more than static electricity. Upon closer inspection, I saw other spirits in the lab, too. In fact, dozens of them. But most were nothing more than faint balls of light.

"Ah, here we go," said Dr. Sculler, who was busy clicking away on his computer. "Caesar Marquez, boxer, age twenty-five, head injury."

"You examined him personally?" I asked.

Sculler nodded gravely. Cutting dead people open was, after all, serious business. "Yes, performed it myself."

"How long have you been a medical examiner, Dr. Sculler?"

"Twenty-two years."

"How many fatally injured boxers?"

"Just the one, although I've seen my share of brain injuries. Particularly football injuries."

"Was Caesar Marquez's brain similarly injured?"

"I'm scanning the autopsy images now, if you would like to look."

"I would."

"Then come around here."

I hadn't worked for the federal government long, but I had seen my share of medical examining rooms and corpses. And these days, death was something to analyze, not to fear. No, never again to fear.

There were dozens of images of a dead man in various stages of examination. The young man, from all appearances, was the same Caesar Marquez I had seen fighting in the YouTube clip.

As I leaned in behind Sculler, he clicked over to a cluster of photographs that focused on the man's head. A few clicks later and the top half of the skull had been removed. The skin itself had been peeled down over the face. The next image showed, from all appearances, a very healthy brain. Finally, the brain had been removed and was now sitting in a small metal tray.

Dr. Sculler zoomed in on the freshly-removed brain that had been housed in a perfectly functioning young adult male just a few hours earlier. Sculler pointed to the screen, in particular to a red discoloration along the left temporal lobe.

"Bleeding," he said. "The brain is susceptible to bleeding, especially after trauma. Unlike other body parts, however, when the brain bleeds, it's a major problem. Bleeding in the brain causes pressure. Pressure can shut down various functions of the brain...and can lead to death. Often quickly."

I said, "The official cause of death is epidural hematoma."

"Yes." He pointed to the screen. "Bleeding between the dura mater and the skull."

"A brain hemorrhage."

"Yes, but in this case the damage is technically classified as an extra-axial hemorrhage, or an intracranial hemorrhage."

I nodded, taking this in. More and more it was looking like Russell Baker didn't have much of a case. "Did you actually see the fight, doctor?"

"I did, yes. Later."

"And did you see enough to warrant a brain hemorrhage?"

The good doctor removed his glasses. As he did so, a spirit of an elderly woman materialized behind him in the far corner of the office. The skin on the doctor's forearms immediately cropped into goose bumps. He shivered slightly, oblivious to the sudden source of cold air. The old woman only partially manifested, hovering on legs that didn't exist. If the good doctor could see what I was seeing, he would undoubtedly run for the hills.

For now, he only shivered, blissfully unaware of the spirit energy around him. The woman faded just as quickly as she appeared. The hollow look in her eyes would have been haunting, if not so familiar. At least, familiar to me.

After shivering some more, he said, "Quite frankly, no."

I perked up. I just hate taking money from a client and then giving them nothing in return.

"No?"

"No. But that doesn't mean that any punch at any point in the fight couldn't have caused the injury. Very little is understood about brain injuries."

"I understand, but is it your professional opinion that you think nothing in the fight warranted death?"

"Not professional. Personal. Unofficial." He paused. "Officially, he died from a blunt force received during the fight."

"Officially, but not likely."

He stared at me, and then started nodding. "Not likely."

"How old was the wound?" I asked.

"It was within the correct time frame. I have no doubt that it happened in and around the time of the fight."

"Or possibly before?" I suggested.

The good doctor shrugged and rubbed his arms. After all, the old lady had reappeared in the far corner of the room.

"Possibly," he said.

9.

It took a few calls, a little waiting, a few more calls, and maybe a little begging to finally meet my next interview.

I met Ricardo Cortez at the Hard Rock Hotel's massive, central bar, where we sat across from each other and nursed our drinks. Mine was white wine. His was a beer. Both of our glasses were small. Around us were the sounds of money being won and lost. Mostly lost.

"You were the referee for the Baker/Marquez fight," I said.

He looked down into his beer. I suspected he often looked down into his beer for answers. That I quickly ascertained he was an alcoholic no longer surprised me. That I felt his overwhelming need and addiction to the stuff did surprise me.

It was almost as if I could reach inside his thoughts.

Almost.

Weeks ago, Hanner had told me that I could expect to start reading other minds—and not just those closest to me. And not just read.

Manipulate.

Jesus.

For now, I didn't want to think about manipulating another's mind—hell, it was all I could do to exist comfortably in my own.

Finally, Ricardo looked up from his beer. He said, "Yes."

"How long have you been a referee?"

"Eight years."

"Have you ever refereed a bout where a fighter was killed?"

Ricardo was a strong-looking Hispanic with what appeared to be the beginning of a tattoo under the right sleeve of his jacket. It looked like a snake tail. In fact, I was certain it was a rattle. We were mostly alone at the bar. Then again, the bar was so expansive that it was hard to tell where it ended and where it started. Nearby, a woman jumped up and down at the nickel slot machine. I think she'd just won a shitload of nickels.

Ricardo ignored the excited woman. Instead, he lifted his beer to his lips, and while he was guzzling he gestured for the waiter for another. Yeah, he was an alcoholic.

When he finally pulled away, he said, "That was my first death."

"Hard on you?"

"What do you think?"

"I'm thinking it was a shitty day for everyone."

"Yup."

The waitress set another beer before him, and Ricardo picked it up instantly.

I said, "Do you blame yourself for his death?"

"No one else to blame."

"What about the guy doing the punching?"

Ricardo shook his head. "It was my job to stop the fight before it gets to that point."

"Except it was a fluke punch. Everyone agrees. Most people think the fight was pretty even up to that point."

"No, it wasn't."

I blinked. This was new information. Investigators loved new information. New information meant that an investigator was onto something. I liked that.

"How so?" I asked.

Ricardo rubbed his face and I saw the scarring on his own knuckles. Ah, he had been a fighter himself. In fact, now I could see that his nose had undoubtedly been broken a few times. Probably not a very good fighter. Probably why he went into reffing fights instead of participating in them. Reffing was easier on the nose.

When he had collected his thoughts and had decided just how much to tell me—and how I knew this was beginning to trouble me—he said, "Caesar was not all there from the beginning."

"What do you mean?"

"Caesar looked, at least to me, that he'd already gone a round or two. Or maybe even three or four."

"Anyone else notice this?"

"Hard to say. I'm certain someone on his crew would have known."

"How could they miss it?"

"Easy to miss, unless you know what to look for."

"And you know what to look for?" I said.

"Of course. All good refs do. It's how we keep these guys from beating in each others' skulls."

"What do you look for?"

Ricardo was loosening up, forgiving himself, reminding himself that there might be more to this story than he knew. Again, how I knew this snippet of thought from him was seriously beginning to wig me out.

He said, "If you know a fighter, it's easier. Then you know their mannerisms. You also know how much punishment they can take."

"You ever work a fight with Caesar?"

"Yup. Two."

"And he was different from the get-go."

"Right. From the fucking get-go."

"What was he doing different?"

"Dazed. Slower than normal."

"Even though most judges scored it even?"

"I said slower than normal. Caesar Marquez was

better than most. I even caught him staggering once or twice back to the corner. Not sure if anyone else had seen it."

"What did you think about that?"

"I thought that something was wrong."

"Enough to stop the fight?"

He shook his head and remembered the beer. He said, "I should have stopped it if I'd had any balls. I should have at least called one of the doctors over. But..."

"But you just weren't sure."

He looked at me funny, as I had read his thoughts. "Right, I wasn't sure. There was no reason for his symptoms, after all. The fight had been fairly tame."

"But he was in trouble from the beginning."

Ricardo nodded. "Almost as if..."

He couldn't finish the sentence, and so I finished it for him. "Almost as if he'd been hurt before the fight."

Ricardo looked at me again. "Bingo."

"Hard to blame yourself for something like this."

"Hard not to, either. I should have stopped the fight."

"You did your best."

He shook his head, and kept on shaking his head even as he finished his second beer and held up his hand for a third.

10.

With Criss Angel in town, I figured something as mundane as a giant flying vampire bat would go unnoticed.

And so I stood on the ledge of my fifteen-floor balcony at the MGM Grand, one of the few hotels in Vegas with open balconies. It was perfect for viewing the Vegas skyline from...or leaping from.

Don't try this at home, kids.

The hot desert wind buffeted my naked body. My longish hair snapped behind me horizontally. Standing naked on a balcony's edge was liberating. Despite being perpetually cold and despite the hot desert wind, I shivered slightly.

After all, the wind was blowing where, as they say, the sun don't shine.

I looked down at the city. An image of the young boxer collapsing in the ring came to me as I stood there. No surprise. This was the city where he'd died, where his autopsy had been conducted, and where I was beginning to suspect he had possibly been killed.

And not by Russell Baker.

Whether or not Caesar Marquez's death was an accident—or something else—remained to be seen.

I didn't need a psychic hit to know that something screwy was going on here. Something wasn't right. What exactly, I didn't know. Maybe I would never know.

I tilted my head back and spread my arms and deeply inhaled the heated desert air—air that was suffused with something that smelled suspiciously like all-you-can-eat $1.99 BBQ ribs.

I stood like that for some time, and the longer I did so, the more I was certain of one thing: I was becoming less and less human.

And more and more something else.

One of them.

I knew this because no human stood on the ledge of their hotel balcony, with arms spread, head tilted back, naked as the day they were born, reveling in their freedom, knowing that an even greater freedom was about to come. A freedom from gravity.

As I stood there, the wind whipping my hair into a frenzy, I wasn't thinking of my kids or Kingsley or Fang or anyone. In fact, I wasn't thinking at all. I was only *feeling*, only *sensing*.

The wind, the heat, the smells, the sounds.

I felt elemental. Animalistic.

I didn't feel like a mother or a friend or a lover. I didn't feel human. I felt, instead, deeply connected to the Earth, a part of the Earth, a part of its elements, its raw material.

I tilted my head forward, knowing that I had to either jump or go back inside. Sooner or later, the cops would be beating down my door. A naked woman on a balcony's ledge was bound to draw some attention.

And I sure as hell wasn't going back in.

The flame appeared in my thoughts. A single, unwavering flame, and within the flame was a creature that should have looked hideous to me, but didn't. It was a creature I felt an extreme fondness for. A love for.

It was, after all, me. In a different shape.

A very different shape.

I lowered my arms and looked down. There was nothing to hinder my drop. No buttresses or projecting balconies.

Just a straight drop.

And so I did just that, tilting forward away from the ledge.

Dropping.

11.

As I fell, as the warm desert wind thundered over me, the winged creature in the flame rushed toward me, filling my thoughts.

I shuddered violently—but kept my eyes closed as I continued to plummet.

I was bigger now, I could feel it, but I hadn't yet fully transformed. I didn't dare open my eyes, knowing the closing of my eyes, the flame, the image...and faith were all part of this process.

I continued to fall, knowing my body was changing rapidly. Metamorphosing. I also knew that the speed of my metamorphosis was contingent on the circumstance. A shorter drop would result in a faster transformation.

Now, I could feel my arms growing, elongating,

feel my body becoming something greater than it was before. Denser, heavier. My awareness of my own body expanded instinctively, exponentially.

I was no longer what I was.

No, I was something much, much bigger.

Much greater.

My wings snapped taut, catching the air, manipulating air, using the air, and now I wasn't so much falling as angling.

I opened my eyes.

Before me stretched the Vegas Strip, in all of its glittering, neon, sinful glory. I flapped my wings hard, instinctively, gaining altitude. Instinctively.

Keeping to the shadows in a city that never sleeps and never turns off was no easy task. And so I took it up another hundred feet or so, flapping my wings, catching hot drafts of sinful air. Yes, the wind was warm and dry and not very different from the air in southern California. That would change in a few months. In a few months, Las Vegas would go from temperate to nuclear.

Too hot for even the undead.

I flapped my wings casually, cruising above the glittering city. I circled once around the superheated laser beam emitting from the Luxor. I continued on, moving north over a cluster of world-famous hotels. The Bellagio with its intricate fountains, the Paris and its Eiffel Tower replica, the Mirage and its gardens, Treasure Island with its pirate ship.

And one flying monster. I wondered idly if the Excalibur needed a real-life dragon. It could supplement my income.

So far, people weren't pointing into the sky and scattering like frightened rabbits before a hawk's shadow. That was a good thing, I guess.

I caught a warm updraft and spread my wings wide and hovered high above the city of sin, staring down, using my supernaturally-enhanced vision to see not only the multitudes crowding the sidewalks, but their actual expressions. Most looked tired. Most looked drunk. There were many groups of young people, no doubt celebrating twenty-first birthdays. A handful of older types wore shorts and T-shirts and sandals. One woman was walking through the crowd bare-chested, high as kite, although not as high as *this* kite. People stopped and stared at her breasts, but for the most part, she was ignored.

Welcome to Vegas.

I saw young men handing out flyers to strip clubs. Most people tossed the flyers aside, which cluttered sidewalks and gutters, pushed along by the warm spring breeze.

I had seen enough of the lights, the gaudy hotels, the plaid tourist shorts, the filth, the degradation, the glitter—and beat my massive wings as hard as I could and shot up into the night sky. I continued flapping them, forcing the rapidly-cooling air down below me. I rose higher and higher, so high that Vegas itself was nothing more than a pinprick of light.

A *bright* pinprick of light, but a pinprick

nonetheless.

Here, on the outer edges of the atmosphere, where little or no oxygen existed, I flapped idly, serenely, holding my position. My mind was mostly empty. Mostly. Images of Kingsley flitted through. Of my son with his growing strength. Of my daughter who seemed to understand that something very strange was happening in the Moon household.

I would have to tell her, too, I thought. *Tell them both. Everything.*

Up here, far above Earth, it was easy to forget that I was a mother, that I had responsibilities. Up here, high above the Earth, it was easy to forget who I was. Up here, drifting on jet-streams and updrafts, buoyed by winds unfelt and unknown by anything living, it was easy to forget I had once been human.

The wind was cold. But not so cold as to affect me in any way. I merely acknowledged the cold, like a scientist noting the cancerous effects of the latest sugar substitute in lab rats.

I spread my wings wide and rode the wind, rising and falling, listening to it thunder over my ears and flap the leathery membranes that were my wings. I did this for an unknowable amount of time, hovering high above the Earth, correcting my altitude ever-so-slightly with minute adjustments to my wings, turning my wrists this way and that, angling my arms this way and that.

This way and that, adjusting, correcting, hovering.

Later, I tucked my wings in and shot down, aiming for the bright speck of light, perhaps the brightest speck of light ever.

Las Vegas.

12.

I alighted on the balcony.

There, I merged with the serious-looking, dark-haired woman in the flame and, after a moment of slight disorientation, found myself standing naked again on the balcony of the MGM Grand Hotel. I often wondered what the transformation process looked like to an outsider. Did I contort and jerk like they do in the movies? Or did I transform in a blink of an eye? I always sensed that my transformation took only a few seconds, but since my eyes were always closed and focused on the flame, I would probably never know. Maybe I would transform for Kingsley one night.

Yeah, I'm a freak.

I donned the white robe I had left draped over

the railing and stepped back into my room. I was just tying the terrycloth belt when I paused. My inner alarm didn't necessarily go off, but it perked up. A slight buzzing just inside my ear.

Someone's here, I thought.

A shape appeared in my thoughts, something glowing—and it appeared, I was sure, directly behind me.

I was moving in an instant, turning, swooping low to the ground, and slammed into whoever was behind me so hard that I drove him into the drywall.

There, I held them up while plaster dust rained down over his shoulders and down onto my raised forearms.

A man. A very beautiful man.

Who gazed down at me with a bemused expression. He was, of course, not a man at all. He was an angel. My one-time guardian angel now turned rogue, so to speak.

I eased my grip and Ishmael dropped lightly to the floor. He shook his head and dust and smaller chunks of wall fell from his long, silver hair and broad shoulders. "Do you greet all your guests this way, Samantha?"

I dusted off my own arms. "Well, let's just say I haven't had a lot of luck in hotel rooms."

If not for a slight prickling of my inner alarm, I would have been completely off-guard. And these days, with my ever expanding extra-sensory perception, someone catching me off-guard was getting harder and harder to do. Unless, of course, that someone was a rogue angel, who seemed to be making a habit of catching me unaware.

"Not as unaware as you might think, Samantha," he said. Unlike other immortals, Ishmael had access to my thoughts. No surprise there, since he'd been my one-time guardian angel. He finished dusting himself off and looked at me. "For the first time, you sensed me nearby. That's quite an accomplishment, and a credit to your growing powers."

Still, I didn't like the implications of that statement. "So you're around me often?"

"What can I say, Samantha? Old habits die hard."

"So, you're often around me?" I repeated, digesting this news.

He nodded. "Myself, and others."

"What others?"

"You know some of them."

"Sephora," I said, recalling the entity I had communicated with last year through automatic writing.

"Yes. Her and others like her."

"Spirit guides," I said, recalling one of my conversations with Sephora.

"Spirit guides, deceased relatives, angels. What some would call your soul group."

"And you."

"Not officially," he said. "Not anymore."

"Not since you fell."

His eyes flashed briefly. "Not since I *chose* a

different path."

Although I couldn't read his thoughts—which seemed damned unfair to me—I could clearly see his aura. And it pulsated around, intermixed with rich color...and deep blackness.

What had once been pure white light—loving light—was now being slowly overrun with coils of blackness so deep that it gave even me the creeps. Even now, something dark and slithery wound around his narrow torso. I watched, fascinated, as it worked its way, around and around, to eventually plunge into his heart region. I was reminded of something monstrous rising up from the ocean depths, something that had no business seeing the light. I shuddered.

"I repulse you," he said. The sadness in his voice was obvious.

"What gave it away?" I said.

I suddenly wanted a cigarette. *Needed* a cigarette. I headed over to my purse, found the pack of Virginia Slims, and lit up.

Ishmael watched my every move closely. I sensed that he was used to watching me closely. That he had always watched me closely. From either afar, or nearby. He had been, after all, my guardian angel.

Of course, I use that term loosely.

That he failed his job miserably was an understatement. That he had done so purposefully was reprehensible.

"Reprehensible is such a strong word, Samantha," he said. "I needed you to be immortal. It was, after all, the only way we could be together."

"You put me in harm's way. You put my kids in harm's way. You put anyone who ever crosses paths with me in harm's way."

"Only if you do not learn to control who you are, Samantha."

"And I suppose you're just the one to teach me?"

"I can help you, Sam."

"Didn't you cause this mess?"

"I did it for love—"

"Shove it," I said, shaking my head.

His clothing, I noted, seemed to shift in color. One moment, his slacks were beige, then brown, then tan. Or maybe I was just going crazy.

"Not crazy, Sam. My clothing is an illusion, of course."

"Of course. That doesn't sound crazy at all."

I exhaled, and looked at him through the churning cigarette smoke. He was a beautiful man. Perhaps the most beautiful I'd ever seen. Too beautiful.

"And what about the rest of you?" I asked.

"Illusion, of course. But I see I have chosen a favorable form."

"Why are you here?"

He continued smiling, and the darkness that swarmed around him—the black snakes and worms and creepy-crawly things—seemed to grow in numbers. It was as if I was seeing evil multiplying before my very eyes. Deepening, propagating. I shivered.

"I'm here to give you news of your dog."

I looked at him sharply. He was, of course, referring to Kingsley. "What about him?"

"He's not a very loyal dog, now is he?" Ishmael smiled broadly. Wickedly.

"What the fuck do you mean?"

"When the vampire's away, the dog shall play."

I brought the cigarette up to my lips, but instead of inhaling, crumpled it in my hands. The temporary burn made me gasp, but the pain faded quickly. "You're lying."

He said nothing, only watched me from the deep shadows of my room, looking supremely pleased.

I looked at my hand. The red mark in the center of my palm was already fading. I threw the remnants of the cigarette over to the closest ashtray. It missed.

"You're trying to drive a wedge between us," I said.

"I didn't have to try very hard, Samantha."

I sensed the not-so-hidden meaning in his words. "You set him up," I said. "Planted someone."

"Call it what you want, Sam. But your doggie took the bait."

"Who is she?"

"Does it matter?"

A familiar sickness appeared in my stomach. Re-appeared. It was a sickness that had nothing to do with the supernatural, a sickness I had lived with for many, many years with Danny. I rubbed my temples and took lots of slow, deep breaths, and when I moved my hand away, I was alone in the hotel room, but I sensed the angel was near. Always near.

The son-of-a-bitch.

13.

It was early afternoon and something was wrong.

I'd been feeling it all day. The forty-five minute plane ride from Vegas to Ontario had seemed like an eternity. Now, driving home from the airport, an inexplicable fear gripped me. Something was seriously wrong.

Except I didn't know what.

My kids, I thought, pressing the gas harder. *Something with my kids.*

But what?

I didn't know. Not yet.

Having extrasensory perception had its benefits, but also its pitfalls. Being keenly aware that something was wrong, but not knowing what, was, if anything, torture.

A moment later, as the dread in me grew to a fever pitch, my cell phone rang. It was my sister, of course.

My kids.

A car blasted its horn next to me. I jumped, jerking my wheel. I had inadvertently swerved into its lane. It continued honking at me even as I snatched up the phone and made an inhuman sound. A squeak, of some sort.

My kids, of course, were staying with their Aunt Mary Lou.

"Mary Lou," I gasped, pressing the phone hard into my ear. "What's wrong?"

"How—never mind." She swallowed. "It's Tammy."

"What about Tammy? What's wrong?" My voice had reached a very loud, shrill note.

"She ran away, Sam."

I took in a lot of worthless air. I had expected worse, true. Running away wasn't the worst, granted, but it wasn't good either. Tammy was, after all, only ten years old.

"When did she leave?"

Mary Lou explained that Tammy had been grumpy all day, irritable. I nodded to myself as Mary Lou spoke. Yes, I'd been noticing this lately, too, although I had chalked it up to her going through some life changes. My sister had assumed Tammy was in her guest room all day, either reading or on the phone. Later, Anthony came out of the very same room and asked where Tammy was. They searched the house and called her cell phone. Her phone was turned off. And that's when Mary Lou called me.

"Did anyone see her leave?"

"No, but we're pretty sure she went out the back door, then through the side gates."

"Did she take a bike?"

"All the bikes are here."

"Did you hear a car pull up front?"

"No, but we weren't paying a lot of attention to the front of the house."

Shit.

Although I didn't have access to my own children's thoughts, that didn't mean they completely escaped my extra-sensory perception, which was why I had sensed something was wrong, and why I had seen the dark halo around Anthony last year, when he had been critically ill.

As my minivan's speedometer climbed past 110 mph, I told Mary Lou I would be there soon and hung up. I focused on keeping the minivan from flipping over.

And keeping myself together.

14.

On my way to my sister's house, I called three of Tammy's closest friends. No one had seen her or heard from her, although everyone pledged to do all they could to help me find her.

I also made another call, to an investigator who had a reputation for tracking down the missing, and as I pulled up to my sister's house in Fullerton, a nondescript Camry was pulling up just behind me.

Spinoza was a small man with a heavy aura. Not a dark aura. Just heavy. Something was eating away at him, making his life a living hell. I didn't need to be psychic to know that he'd lost something important to him.

Spinoza parked on the street behind me and got out. He was a small man. The complete opposite of

Kingsley or the beast, Knighthorse. And as Spinoza came toward me, concern creasing his pleasantly handsome face, I suddenly had a whiff of something that made me nearly vomit.

The scent of burned flesh.

Sweet Jesus, I thought, as I saw in my mind's eye a burned hand and twisted metal and broken glass.

His son's hand. There had been an accident. Mixed with the smell of burnt flesh was alcohol. Spinoza, I was suddenly certain, had been driving. Drunk.

Sweet Jesus, I thought again.

Spinoza took my hand and as he did so, the psychic vision and smell of burning flesh disappeared. He next gave me a small, awkward hug. The look in his eyes was one of only concern. I suddenly suspected why Spinoza was known for finding the missing, especially missing children.

"How you holding up?" he asked.

"Been better. Thanks for coming out on short notice."

He nodded. "We'll find her, Sam. Don't worry." And his quiet strength and assuredness spoke volumes. It also calmed me down. Somewhat.

I led the way into my sister's house, where Detective Sherbet of the Fullerton Police Department was already inside. No, I wasn't too concerned that a homicide investigator was there since I had called him, too. Detective Sherbet had become a good friend. So good, in fact, that he and I now shared a deepening telepathic link. Granted, the good detective wasn't exactly thrilled by our telepathic link, but he seemed to be getting the hang of it.

We'll find her, Sam, he thought, nodding, his words appearing softly just inside my ears.

Thank you, Detective.

Mary Lou came over next with tears in her eyes, looking so distraught that I was the one doing the reassuring. "Not your fault," I said over and over as she completely broke down.

Once she'd gotten control of herself, I planned our course of action with the detectives. At ten years old, Tammy would have fewer choices available to her. She couldn't drive and she didn't have a lot of money. She wasn't addicted to drugs and didn't have a boyfriend. At least, as far as I knew.

Truth was, I had a hard time getting a psychic handle on my own kids. I could read their auras, but that was about it. It was the same with my sister and with her kids; and the same with my parents, although these days I didn't see them very often.

Mary Lou had confirmed that some toiletries were missing, along with her gym bag. We even confirmed that a jar of peanut butter and some saltines were gone, too. Tammy's favorite snack.

Still, a child walking the streets alone with a gym bag was trouble, and it was all I could do to stay calm. Running outside and screaming for my baby wouldn't help anything, although that's exactly what I felt like doing.

Easy, Sam, came Sherbet's words. *A child walking around with a gym bag would just as easily get the attention of police. And I have my best men out there looking for her.*

"Does she have a cell phone?" Spinoza asked. We were grouped around Mary Lou's living room.

"It's off," I said.

Spinoza and Sherbet winced. We all knew that a phone had to be on to be used as a tracking device.

"Laptop or tablet computer?" pressed Spinoza. "Anything with GPS?"

I shook my head. "No."

"Does she know anyone with a car?"

"She'd better not."

"Does she have access to a bike? Anything she can move quickly on?"

"The bikes are at home."

Spinoza glanced over at my sister. "And all bikes are accounted for here?"

"Yes. Bikes and skateboards."

I was having a hard time concentrating, focusing, and remembering what I should do in an investigation like this. *But it's not an investigation,* I thought. *It's my daughter—and she's gone.*

Sherbet glanced at me again and then looked over at my sister. "Do you have any recent pictures of Tammy?"

"I do, yes. On my cell phone."

"Can you print me out a half dozen?"

She nodded eagerly and dashed off to where I

knew her husband had his own office at home.

While she was gone, we finalized our plan. Sherbet would work with the local beat cops and cruise the streets in a coordinated effort. Spinoza would hit every Starbucks, fast-food restaurant and store within two square miles. I would contact all her friends and head straight to all her known hangouts.

Mary Lou came back with the color photos. Seeing her photo, with her happy, smiling face made me almost lose it right there.

Easy, Sam, came Sherbet's soothing voice.

The detective next instructed Mary Lou to email the same image to his department. An APB had already been sent to all units with a description of my daughter, including her current, assumed clothing. Now they would have a corresponding photo.

It's real, I thought, listening to Sherbet instruct his department. *She's really missing.*

I fought to control my breathing. To control myself. Finally, Sherbet clicked off his phone.

"That's all we can do on this end," said Sherbet, turning to us. "Let's hit the streets."

15.

After we split up, I sat briefly in my minivan, searching for a psychic hit that wasn't there. Despite the many abilities I'd been given, a psychic connection to my own kids was not one of them.

For now, I was just a mom with a missing daughter.

I had just put the vehicle into gear, mentally going through a list of her friends and where they lived, when my cell phone rang. I gasped and swerved a little and reached for my cell.

Kingsley Fulcrum.

Shit.

I switched on my Bluetooth. "Hey."

"Sam! I just got your text. Have you found her?"

I had indeed sent him a text, but now I regretted doing so. Kingsley Fulcrum was the last person I wanted to think about now.

"Not yet," I said, as I turned right onto Commonwealth. My sister lived closer to downtown than I did. People were everywhere. I scanned the streets.

"I'm coming out now. Where are you?"

"No," I said. "Don't come."

"What—"

"I sent you that text an hour ago. Where were you?"

He paused only briefly, but tellingly. "I was with a client."

"I'm sure you were, big guy. And don't worry, we've got it handled."

"Sam—wait! Are you saying you don't want my help?"

"That's what I'm saying," I said.

"Sam—"

But I had already clicked off.

I sat back and gripped the wheel and wound slowly through downtown Fullerton, knowing that I could have used Kingsley's help, and knowing that I was allowing the hurt in my own heart to possibly get in the way of such help.

But I just couldn't see him. Or talk to him.

Not now. Perhaps not ever.

16.

I tried her cell phone for the tenth time.

And for the tenth time, it went straight to voicemail. Her voicemail message was the generic electronic one. I didn't even get the benefit of hearing her little voice.

I even checked once or twice to make sure I was calling the right number. Crazy, I know. It said "Tammy" right here in the "Contacts" list, the same Tammy I had called countless times since she had first gotten her cell last Christmas.

I set the phone in my lap, confirmed it was on, and realized that my brain was spinning, looping over the same things again and again. As soon as I set the phone in my lap, I wanted to pick it up again, and try her cell phone. Again.

Again and again.

Deep breaths, Sam.

Yes, I could have used Kingsley's help. Hell, I could use Fang's help, too. And Knighthorse's and Aaron King's and anyone else I'd ever come across.

Deep breaths, Sam.

She's not far. Ten-year-old girls eventually get picked up by the police—

Or picked up by other people. Scumbags. Dirt bags. Killers. Child molesters.

Now I was panicking all over again and stomping the gas and whipping through suburban Fullerton as if it was my own private race course.

I ended up at home, which was about three miles from my sister's home. I parked the van at an angle in front of the house, dashed out, hurdled the chain-link fence that surrounded the property, and plunged inside my house, calling her name.

No response.

I quickly scoured every room. My hope had been that she simply returned to her own home, her own room, her own bed. Still, I called her name repeatedly, searching everywhere and anywhere, even out in the garage. I moved quickly through the house. I sped around supernaturally quickly. The rooms and walls and carpet were a blur. Pictures were a blur. My head was spinning.

I caught myself on a wall.

I gasped, chest heaving. Having a full-blown panic attack wouldn't help anyone, least of all, my daughter. I knew this. I had cautioned parents of this very thing many times in the past, when searching for their own runaways.

Deep breaths, Sam. Calm down.

Fuck calming down. I want my daughter.

Shaking, I stood straight, hands on hips, thinking hard. Or trying to think hard. Truth was, my brain still hadn't entirely kicked into gear. Night was coming, but was not here yet.

I hated what I was sometimes. Hated it. Here I needed to find my daughter, and I needed to think *clearly,* but I couldn't push past the fog.

I paced and checked the time on my cell. One more hour until sundown. Then I would think clearly. Perhaps even get a psychic hit or two.

Except one hour might be too late.

My phone rang. I gasped, and nearly dropped it. Kingsley. Again. The asshole. The fucker. How dare he call me when he knew I was waiting to hear news about my daughter.

I ignored it. He tried one more time. I ignored that, too, hating him more and more.

I had tried her closest friends. Sherbet was cruising the streets with his patrol officers. Spinoza was hitting any and all shops within a reasonable radius.

How much money did she have?

I thought hard, forcing my mind to go back a few days, before my trip to Vegas. Yes, I had given her and Anthony $20 each. A twenty wasn't much.

I gripped my keys and turned for the door, nodding to myself. Twenty bucks was just enough for—

My phone rang again.

It was Spinoza.

I paused and clicked on, pressing the touch screen so hard I nearly cracked it. "Any news?" I asked. Or tried to ask. My voice cracked and sounded funny, even to my ears.

"Very good news, Sam," he said gently. "I've got someone here you might be interested in seeing."

"Oh, God," I said and sank to my knees.

"She's with me, Sam. Safe and sound. We're at the bus station in Buena Park. Do you know the one?"

I buried my face in my hands, pressing the phone against my ear. "Yes."

"We'll be here waiting."

I clicked off and let the tears flow, sitting there on my knees, my face in my hands.

17.

They were eating ice cream together on a bus bench.

Buena Park's Park and Ride was a big station, perhaps the biggest in north Orange County, too big for a little girl to be sitting alone.

I parked just behind the benches, where I could see Tammy and Spinoza, both happily munching on their ice creams. Tammy was swinging her legs. I could just make out Mary Lou's gym bag sitting next to her.

With the 5 Freeway roaring above, choked with rush hour traffic, and Orangethorpe Avenue opposite, nearly as busy, no one would have noticed a screaming girl being yanked into someone's car, never to be seen or heard from again.

I inhaled slowly, deeply.

But there she was, safely eating ice cream with Spinoza as if she knew the man. She didn't, of course. She had never met the investigator, and yet, there she was eating ice cream with him. So trusting. So innocent. He could have been anyone. Someone dangerous. Someone with not very good intentions. He wasn't dangerous, of course. He was a damn fine investigator. But she didn't know that.

Spinoza turned and saw me sitting in my van. Perhaps he was psychic himself. He waved, holding his ice cream. There was a vending machine nearby. No doubt it had been the source of the frozen dessert.

I sat in my car and waited for my heart to calm down, for my breathing to calm down, and, as I waited, never once did I take my eyes off my daughter.

***

Spinoza got up and pulled me aside as I approached.

"You know the drill," said Spinoza quietly. He was only a few inches taller than me. His height always surprised me. My memory of him was always as a bigger man.

I nodded, knowing where this was going.

The evening was giving way to dusk, and the lights in the bus stop were turning on. Tammy kicked her feet...and looked away. So far, she hadn't made eye contact with me. She was dressed in jeans and T-shirt. She had on a pink belt. She was too damn cute to be alone at a bus station.

"She thinks you're going to be mad at her," he said.

I nodded. It's the same speech I gave parents myself, after finding their own runaways.

"She's also angry."

I snapped my head around. "Angry?"

Spinoza gave me a wry smile. "Life's unfair and all that. You know, typical girl stuff."

I nodded, relieved, although I wasn't sure about that "girl stuff" comment.

He continued, "Sherbet's on his way, too, so you'll have a few minutes alone with her. I tried to call him off, but he has to follow up, access the situation, finalize a report, and call off the hounds, so to speak."

I nodded, looked at Spinoza. "How did you know she was here?"

"A hunch. I listen to them."

I suddenly gave him a hug which, I think, surprised the hell out of him, although it shouldn't have. He was lucky I didn't give him a smooch, too.

"I do, too," I said, releasing him. "Except this time I couldn't think straight."

"Hard to think straight when your kid's gone," he said, and now there was no mistaking the sorrow in his voice. I knew his own kid was gone. Long gone. He nodded toward Tammy. "Talk to her, Sam. Gently."

I said I would. He smiled and nodded and touched my elbow awkwardly, then slipped out into the night.

I turned to Tammy.

18.

"Hey, booger butt," I said, sliding next to her.

She turned her face away. "I'm not a booger butt."

The hem of her jeans were rolled up, exposing her pink socks and cute tennis shoes. She was wearing a pink Hello Kitty T-shirt. The purse sitting next to the handbag was also Hello Kitty. The gym bag was my sister's. She continued kicking feet that didn't quite touch the gum-covered cement ground.

"Then what are you?" I asked, knowing it was a leading question.

"A young lady. A woman."

"A woman?" I said and it was all I could do to not laugh. She looked at me sharply and I literally swallowed my laughter as surely as if I'd swallowed food. *Liquid food*, of course.

"Yes, a woman," she said, sticking her chin out. A sharp chin. Danny's chin.

"I see. Well, I thought women were, in the very least, teenagers."

"No, Mom. That's why they're called teenagers."

It was all I could do not to point out that she herself was still three years shy of being a teenager. I said, "So, you're a young lady now."

"Yes."

"More mature than even teenagers."

She made a sort of "as if" noise. That my daughter considered herself superior to teenagers told me a lot about her. It also told me that she was a handful.

I said, "Mature enough to travel alone?"

She shrugged. She still hadn't looked at me. "It's just a bus. Kids take buses every day to school."

"A bus to where?" I asked. I was part amused, part horrified. Jesus, what if she had actually gotten on board the bus? Maybe nothing, actually. Bus drivers were trained not to let kids on board alone, unless Tammy came up with a really good story. She was, after all, a gifted storyteller. I often thought I might have a little writer on my hands.

After all, Tammy was the creator of Lady Tamtam, a crime-fighting superhero mom who could fly and shoot lasers from her eyes.

Lady Tamtam, I was certain, was based on me.

And maybe a little bit of Lady Gaga, too. Except Lady Tamtam fought crime, while Lady Gaga, apparently, had sex with it.

Of course, Lady Tamtam shot lasers from her eyes, which I doubted I could. *Only one way to see.* I focused on an empty Cheetos bag sticking out from a nearby trash can. Nope, no lasers.

Tammy didn't know her mother's super-secret identity. Unless Anthony had spilled the beans. But I didn't think he had. He would have told me. Or I would have heard about it before this.

No, there was something else going on here.

"Tammy," I said, reaching out to her and taking her hand. She resisted at first, but then let me take it. She still wouldn't look at me. "Tammy. Why did you run away?"

I sat like that for a second or two, unmoving, holding her hand. She sat unmoving, too, although she bit her lower lip. A sure sign that she was thinking hard. Finally, she turned and looked at me for the first time, and there were tears in her eyes.

"Because I'm horrible, Mommy."

I squeezed her hand. "Why would you say that?"

Now her lower lip was trembling. "Because I hate Anthony."

"Why do you hate your little brother?"

She shrugged and lowered her head.

"Out with it, young lady."

"He's just such a jerk."

"A jerk, how?"

"I dunno."

"Yes, you do."

"I just hate him."

"Yeah, you said that. He's your little brother. You can't hate your little brother. I forbid it."

She stuck out her bottom lip. Anthony did the same thing, a habit he picked up from his older sister. A sister he idolized growing up. A sister he followed tirelessly.

I waited for her to sort out her thoughts and feelings. And since I couldn't dip into her thoughts, I had to wait just like any other mama.

"He's...different somehow," she finally said.

"So that's why you hate him? Because he's different?"

"No. Not really. Well, kind of."

"Tammy..."

"Everyone talks about him, Mommy. I mean everyone. I'm so damn tired of it."

"Watch your mouth, young lady."

"Sorry."

"Who talks about him, Tammy?"

"Everyone. Everyone at school. Everyone at home. You, dad. Teachers, doctors. I'm just so sick of it."

"So you don't really hate your brother. You're just tired of people talking about him."

"No, I hate him."

"What did he do to you?"

"He's just a butthead."

Despite myself, I laughed, and shortly, Tammy

started giggling. I reached out and tickled her and she laughed even harder, and as we both laughed I saw a pair of headlights appear in the parking lot, then another and another. Three cop cars closed in, with Sherbet in the lead.

I looked at Tammy. "Sweetie, someday we need to talk about something very important."

"I know, Mommy."

I opened my mouth to speak but stopped. I tried again, changing directions. "You know what, baby?"

"About you."

"You know *what* about me?"

"You're special, Mommy."

"Special how?"

She smiled sweetly and said, "You know, Mommy."

As Sherbet appeared, looking red-faced and relieved, I thought of Lady Tamtam and her supernatural powers. The mother who could fly. The mother who fought crime. The mother who shot lasers from her eyes.

Still, two out of three weren't bad.

19.

Russell Baker and I were at a Starbucks in Fullerton.

It was the same Starbucks where I'd met the very creepy Robert Mason, one-time soap opera star, one-time owner of the Fullerton Playhouse, who was now a full-time resident of a jail cell.

My time here with Russell Baker was decidedly more pleasant.

The young boxer was wearing a loose tank top and shorts. He had just finished working out with Jacky. Jacky wasn't his official trainer, but, like many young boxers, they sought his help and considered it an honor to work with the legendary Irishman.

More importantly, Russell looked good in a tank

top. I suspected he would look good in just about anything. Of course, being in shape and looking good was expected from a professional boxer. Still, professional or not, sitting across from me was a very breathtaking man. Even for someone who doesn't need much breath.

I said, "I spoke with Dr. Sculler in Las Vegas."

"The medical examiner," said Russell, sounding very un-boxer-like. He had a quick mind. I only hoped it wouldn't be beaten out of him by the end of his career.

"Right," I said. "The official cause of death is epidural hematoma."

"I know," he said. "I've read the report. A dozen or so times."

Russell was sipping from a bottle of water. Who goes to a Starbucks and orders a bottle of water? Then again, I looked down at my own bottle of water. Well, boxers in training and vampires, apparently. I wondered if we just might be the first two people in the history of Starbucks to only order two bottles of water.

Big picture, Sam.

I continued, "I'll admit it. I thought I was going to come back here and tell you that you don't have a case."

He glanced up at me, blinking. He cocked his head a little. "You *thought*? What does that mean?"

"It means that it's Dr. Sculler's *un*official opinion that you could not have caused the kind of brain damage he saw in the autopsy."

Russell sat up. I knew that this was the kind of news he was praying for. "I..." he paused, gathering his thoughts. "I don't understand."

"Officially, based on probable evidence, Caesar was killed in the ring. After all, he collapsed in front of the world."

Russell nodded.

I went on, "But Dr. Sculler didn't see enough evidence, based on what he saw of the fight, to warrant the scope of damage he saw in Caesar's brain tissue."

"Then why had he reported that it had?"

"Caesar was a boxer. He died of a brain hemorrhage. It's a slam-dunk case for everyone involved. The evidence is obvious. Unless—"

"Unless you look deeper," he finished.

Interesting. That was exactly how I was going to finish the sentence. I wondered again if I was somehow opening myself up to other people. How I was doing that, I didn't know, but I made a mental note to learn to stop it. At any rate, Russell seemed oblivious to the fact that he might have gotten a sneak peek into my thoughts. Into the mind of a vampire. Maybe his oblivion was a good thing.

"Right," I said. "Dr. Sculler also let it be known that he was by no means an expert in boxing-related brain trauma and could not, therefore, give me a true expert's opinion."

"So, a non-expert declared that Caesar's death was boxing related?"

"That's about the extent of it."

"Man, that shit ain't right." He turned away, swearing under his breath. He looked back at me. "I didn't kill him, Sam. Caesar and I were amateurs together. We practiced a few times, sparred together in the early days. That guy could take a punch. That last fight...we were only feeling each other out. I landed maybe one solid punch. One. And even that wasn't my best shot. Caesar could take dozens of those, maybe more."

And that was the crux. How much could one man take before his brain finally gave? How much was too much before a guy collapsed in the ring, dead?

"There's one other thing worth pointing out," I said. "The doctor does not dispute that Caesar suffered an injury that could cause death."

"Just that he didn't think I caused it in the ring."

"Right," I said.

"So, if I didn't hit him hard enough to kill him..."

"Then someone else did."

20.

I was on my way to L.A.

With me was a list of names provided by Russell Baker. On the list were three names: Caesar Marquez's trainer, cut-man and manager, all three of which would have been in Caesar's locker room prior to the fight. And *prior* was key here.

After all, something had happened to Caesar before the fight, something that had directly led to his death. What it was remained to be seen.

As I followed behind an endless sea of red brake lights, my cell rang for perhaps the dozenth time that day. And for the dozenth time that day, I saw that it was Kingsley Fulcrum. This time, as the phone rang, a text message appeared. Virtually simultaneously. I guess the big oaf could multi-task.

The text message read: *Sam, please pick up.*

I thought about ignoring him again, until I realized the hairy bastard would just keep calling me...and since I wasn't in any kind of mood to see him face to face, I thought I might as well hear what he had to say.

The phone rang again and, when it was about to go to voicemail, I picked up.

"It's your dime," I said flippantly.

"Oh, Sam! I was just about to hang up."

"That was valuable information to have. Thank you for sharing."

"Don't be this way, Sam."

"What way?" I asked. "Hurt? Betrayed? How would you suggest I be instead, Kingsley? Ecstatic that a man I was falling in love with fucked another woman?"

"Sam, we need to talk."

"Then talk."

"Not like this. Not over the phone."

"Perhaps in your bed where you fucked her?"

"Sam..."

I waited. I had broken out in a sweat. Many of my human functions had stopped altogether, but sweating was not one of them. I sweated with the best of them, especially in a warm minivan on a long drive to L.A., and dealing with *this*.

Again.

I shook my head, swearing silently. Kingsley and I had been dating over eight months now. I had just started feeling the love again. Had just started letting him in, had just started getting over the pain of my cheating ex.

"Sam," he tried again. "How did you know?"

"Does it matter?"

He must have thought hard about that because he paused good and long. "No. I guess not."

But I knew it was eating at him. Good.

We were silent some more. Traffic on the 5 Freeway was sick. It was midday and I had already made plans for Mary Lou to pick up the kids. I had made special plans to be with Tammy tonight. So had Mary Lou. We were going to have a girl's night out, so to speak. No boys allowed.

"Who was she?" I asked.

"I don't honestly know."

"What do you mean?"

"She just...appeared in the office. Wanted to make an appointment. Flirted with me endlessly. Caught me as I was leaving work for the day. Walked with me out to my car. Laughed at everything I said. Touched me, asked me questions. Then asked if I wanted to get a drink with her."

"And you said yes."

"Yes," said Kingsley. "I did."

"You didn't have to say yes."

"I know, Sam."

"But you did."

"Yes."

"Why?"

There was a lot of silence on his end. I could hear him breathing, each breath pouring over the receiver as if he were in a sporadic windstorm.

"I don't know why, Sam."

"Yes you do. Why?"

"She gave me a lot of attention."

"Lots of women give you attention."

"She was different."

"Prettier."

"Yeah, maybe."

"Prettier than me."

"I didn't say that."

"You didn't have to. So at what point did you fuck her?"

"Sam, how do you know this? Did you plant her?"

And that's when I hung up on him, nearly crushing my cell phone in the process. He cheats on me...and turns it around? The fucker. The piece of shit.

And as I drove into the afternoon sun, feeling eternally exhausted and too hurt for tears, I realized that Kingsley had been partially right.

He *had* been set up. Just not by me.

21.

Caesar Marquez was trained by his brother at the family gym in downtown Los Angeles, which is where I found myself now.

His brother's name was Romero and he and I were walking through the gym together. The gym was not unlike Jacky's gym in Fullerton. The difference, though, was that Jacky catered to teaching women to defend themselves. The Marquez Gym catered to extremely muscular young men who seemed to take delight in punching the crap out of each other.

"We've produced eleven number-one fighters," said Romero. Sounding remarkably like Jacky, he paused to tell a young Hispanic kid, who was working a heavy bag, to keep his gloves up. I thought trainers everywhere were entirely too concerned about gloves being up. Then again, what did I know?

I said, "Must be good for business."

He nodded and we continued on, weaving slowly through the gym. I was, I noted, the only female here. Once or twice I spotted a set of eyes watching me, but mostly, the young fighters kept their heads down and their gloves up.

As we circled a ring where a black guy and a white guy, both wearing head gear, were trading jabs, Romero said, "Caesar would have been the twelfth."

I said, "I'm sorry to hear about Caesar."

Romero nodded again and we watched the two fighters above us. Both fighters were slugging it out. Fists flew, sweat slung. Some of the sweat landed on my forearm. *Eew.*

"My family," began Romero, as I discreetly wiped the sweat off on my jeans, "are all fighters. I was good, but it turns out, I'm a better trainer than a fighter. Caesar, well, he was something else. He was on his way up. Moving fast, too. He was already ranked in the top ten in his weight class. Top ten and moving up."

"How many brothers do you have?"

"Three living, now one dead."

I blinked, astonished. "There were five of you?"

"Yes. Four now. All boxers. Caesar was the youngest and probably the best. Our father started things off by boxing in a few amateur fights back in the day. He was okay but didn't love it enough to pursue it. My oldest brother, Eduard, loved it. Passionately. He was good. That's him over there." He pointed to a stockier version of himself, a guy who was maybe in his mid-forties and was working closely with a young black guy. They were practicing bobbing and weaving drills. I'd done a few of those with Jacky. "Anyway, his passion drove all of us. Especially Caesar."

Romero's voice was steady, his eyes dry. That he was discussing a brother who had passed not even three weeks ago, one would never guess. Then again, his voice was too steady, and he blinked too much. He was doing what he could to control himself. I suspected this was a very macho culture, and brothers who ran a world-class boxing gym were perhaps the most macho of all.

We continued through the gym and, without thinking, I threw a punch at an empty heavy bag. It was still daylight and so, I couldn't put much into the punch, but I think Jacky would have been proud. It had been a straight shot and I had gotten most of my weight behind my punch.

Romero, who had been leading me into his office, just about stumbled over himself. He looked at the bag moving violently back and forth, creaking along its chains. Then he looked at me.

"Do that again," he said.

"Lucky punch," I said, realizing my mistake. I really, really hated drawing attention to myself. What possessed me to punch the bag, I don't know.

Or, maybe a part of me envisioned it being Kingsley.

Or Ishmael.

"Humor me," he said in his thick Spanish accent. "Please."

I gave the punch a half-assed jab.

"No, *chica*. Hit it again. Like you did before. Please."

Screw it, I thought. The cat was already out of the bag, so to speak, and Jacky himself had been secretly spreading the word that he had on his hands a woman who could beat most men. Perhaps even Romero had heard about me through the boxing grapevine.

So, I took a breath, focused on the bag in front of me, bounced on my feet a little, positioned my shoulders the way Jacky had taught me, and punched the bag with all my strength, which, of course, was diminished, due to the time of day. And this time I really did think of Kingsley's face...and this time, the heavy bag did much more than swing and creak on the chain.

It flew forward and up—so hard and fast that it dislodged itself from the hook it was hanging on. Now it was tumbling end over end, to finally come to a rest halfway across the gym. A few boxers had jumped out of the way.

"*¡Ay Dios mio!*" said Romero and he made the sign of the cross.

Many others had turned to watch me. All looked startled. Or, in the very least, confused. Then they all went back to working out and keeping their hands up.

Romero continued to stare at me.

"Oops," I said.

22.

We were in his office, which had a view of most of the gym. Presently, two men were hoisting the heavy bag and repositioning it on the hook. They were using a stepladder and were sweating with effort.

Romero had yet to say anything. He was in his late thirties, extremely fit, and would have been good-looking if not for the fact that he seemed to have a permanent case of cauliflower ear. That was the condition many fighters got when the ear swelled up.

Ah, screw it, I decided. He was still damn good-looking, cauliflower ear and all.

He was leaning back in his office chair, lightly tapping the tips of his fingers together over his chest. The words on his tank top said: *Marquez Gym - Elite Training*.

"You gonna say something," I said, "or just sit there and look at me like I'm a freak."

"I'm sorry, *señorita*," he said, literally shaking his head. "I'm trying to understand what happened out there."

"Sometimes, there are no easy answers."

"I suppose not," he said, then his eyes sort of glazed over a little. I think he was re-living the moment, especially as he began voicing his thoughts. "Good form, good stance, a good punch. A straight shot."

He rubbed his face and looked at me.

I smiled sweetly. "What can I say," I said. "A lucky shot."

"A helluva shot. Or punch. Jacky's been talking about you."

"Jacky exaggerates."

Romero shook his head. I think—*think*—his cauliflower ears might have wobbled a little. "Actually, no, *señorita*. I would say Jacky is not known to exaggerate. If he says a boxer is damn good, the boxer is damn good."

"I'm not a boxer," I said.

Romero raised his eyebrows. "Maybe not, but you can punch."

"I'm not looking for a trainer," I said. "I'm here about your brother."

That snapped him out of whatever reverie he was in. "My brother?"

I nodded. "I'm looking for answers, Romero."

He didn't want to let go of what he'd just seen outside the office—in his own gym, no less—something that defied logic and common sense. He finally looked at me, and he finally showed me his real self. Maybe my little display had broken through his machismo and affected him on a deeper level. I didn't know. But there was a change in him. His walls were coming down and as he looked at me, simply staring at me with an intensity I'd only seen a few times in my life—and perhaps only from Kingsley's hauntingly amber eyes—Romero broke down.

And he broke down hard.

He covered his face with his hand and wept into it, shuddering, his shoulder muscles and triceps rippling. I watched the tears appear through his fingers and cascade down over his knuckles, and watched as his aura rippled with hues of blues and greens.

After a few minutes of this, he rubbed his face with the backs of his hands. "I'm not sure what came over me."

"It's natural," I said. "And perfectly okay."

"It's not natural for me." He wiped his eyes some more. "I miss him so much, Ms. Moon."

"I understand."

"He should not be dead." Romero shook his head, rubbed his arms. "Caesar rarely absorbed punishment. He was good. Damn good. He was the one handing out the beatings. And when he wasn't punching, he was ducking and weaving."

"Tell me about the fight."

"The fight was no different than the rest. Russell Baker's good, but not that good. He must have landed a lucky shot or two, enough to do damage. Hard to say."

"Is it your professional opinion that your brother was hit hard enough to be killed?"

"From what I saw? No. From what I know about boxing? Anything can happen."

"Who's allowed in the locker room before a fight?"

He shrugged. "I guess anyone the fighter allows."

"And who did your brother allow?"

"Myself, my older brother, Eduardo, his manager, his girlfriend, and his promoter."

"That's a lot of people."

"Not really. Mostly Caesar was with me and Eduardo, discussing strategy, last-minute thoughts, and trying to calm him down. He is always so excited before a fight."

"But you were Caesar's official trainer, correct?"

"Yes. But that didn't stop my other brothers from coming in and giving us their two cents worth."

He chuckled. I chuckled. I said, "Was there ever a problem having that many people in the locker room before a fight?"

"Rarely. Call it controlled mayhem."

"Tell me about the locker room on the night in question. Did anything happen that stands out? Anything unusual? Out of the norm?"

He was shaking his head and thinking hard, now running his fingers through his thick, black hair. I noticed some magazines near his computer keyboard. No, not magazines. Travel guides to the Bahamas. "No, sorry. Nothing that stands out."

"You said his girlfriend was in the locker room that night."

"Yes."

"What was his relationship like with his girlfriend?"

Romero shrugged. "Normal, I suppose."

"Define normal."

"They mostly got along."

"Mostly?"

He shrugged again. "They fought like anyone, I guess."

"They fight physically?"

Romero paused and cocked his head a little, giving me a better view of his cauliflower ear. I tried not to make a face. "I'm not sure what you're suggesting, Ms. Moon, but I can assure you that he did not have any altercations with his girlfriend before the fight. I was with him the entire time."

"Did your brother mention if he'd been fighting with his girlfriend earlier? Say at the hotel room?"

Romero looked away and shrugged. "He mentioned a small fight. Nothing big. But they had made up by the time of the fight."

"Prior to the Vegas fight, when was Caesar's last fight?"

Romero looked up, thinking. "Four months ago."

"So three months before his death?"

"Yes."

"How rigorous are his sparring sessions?"

"Rigorous?"

"Yes. Could he have suffered any punishment during practice?"

"We use headgear, Ms. Moon. We go light. Not too heavy. We break up anything that gets too physical."

"Is it your expert opinion that Caesar could not have suffered any real injury in his practices leading up to his last fight?"

"None."

"And he didn't have a history of brain trauma?"

"None. He was just a kid and a damn good fighter. Damn good. He could have been the best."

I nodded, and wondered why I was feeling like I wasn't getting the whole story. Romero was fighting back tears. Caesar was dead, and there was only one obvious lead. I said, "Can I have his girlfriend's information?"

23.

I somehow found a parking spot on the street near Allison Lopez's Beverly Hills apartment. By *near*, I meant three blocks away, all of which I hoofed under the last rays of the setting sun.

Normally I would have been sprinting...and my skin would have been burning and blistering. Even in the setting sun.

But now, all I felt was mildly uncomfortable. No sprinting needed. If anything, I felt like I was coming down with a cold. Or a feeling of weakness. Mild apprehension.

And so, I moved along the tree-lined sidewalk with as much energy as I could muster, knowing that in about twenty minutes, I would have all the energy in the world.

Just twenty more minutes.

I moved between opulent apartments and condo skyrises, some many dozens of stories high, and all boasting glass and steel and smooth plaster. All reflecting the setting sun. Some had limousines parked out front, waiting with doors open, chauffeurs standing ready. I saw no fewer than three Paris Hilton look-a-likes, all texting while their dogs squatted on narrow strips of grass out front. The dogs each looked up at me in unison as I passed, baring their little white teeth. One of them even leaped at me, nearly causing its owner to drop her phone.

Whew!

Dogs didn't like me, which was annoying, since I was a dog lover. But I was especially a wolf lover. Except that thought, of course, depressed me instantly, so I let it go.

At Allison's apartment—one of the bigger and more opulent ones, no less—I followed the instructions as given to me by her during our brief phone conversation just a few minutes earlier.

I pressed the pound button on the caller box but nothing happened. I pressed it again. Nothing. No response. There was no sign that the damned thing was even working. Frustrated, I dialed Allison's cell number; it was busy. Unlike New York apartments, few L.A. apartments have doormen. This one didn't. The plush lobby, just beyond the glass entryway, was empty.

I stood there, frustrated.

I looked around. One of the Paris Hilton look-alikes was still texting, even though her dog had finished piddling minutes ago. I looked over another shoulder. No one.

I looked back at the locked glass door. There was no doorknob, just a handle. A heavy deadbolt fastened the door to a thick metal frame. No doubt, everyone within the building felt safe and secure in their posh apartments, as well they should. This bolt was serious business, released only by the occupants within. The sign above the handle said "Pull."

Two things happened simultaneously. The first was that the sun had finally set. I knew this because I suddenly felt more alive than I ever had before, which is saying something. The second was that the deadbolt tore through the metal door frame, ripping sideways through the metal.

The sound was god-awful loud. I looked casually back to the Paris look-alike. She was still texting, oblivious to life beyond her smart phone screen. I did, however, have the full attention of her little dog.

I wiped the handle clean of my prints, stepped through the doorway, waved to the security camera, and headed over to the elevators, knowing full well that I wasn't wearing enough makeup to even show up on camera.

Sometimes it was good to be me.

24.

Allison answered her door with her own cell phone pressed against her. She waved me in without a thought. I wondered if she was aware that she hadn't actually buzzed me in.

The apartment was smaller than I had expected, but the monthly rent was undoubtedly quadruple my own mortgage. The door opened into a small hallway that led first to a smallish kitchen. Shoe boxes were piled on the counter and spilled over onto some stools, as well. The shoe boxes were printed with Jimmy Choo and Manolo and Valentino, words that were foreign to a single, working mother who lived in the suburbs.

I continued following Allison into a smallish living room, where she motioned offhandedly for me to sit on an oversized couch. I was just figuring out how to offhandedly sit, when I saw something I probably shouldn't have seen.

A fresh cut along the inside of her finger.

Normally, the sight of blood does little for me. Yes, I drink blood. Yes, it nourishes this strange body of mine. But that's about the extent of it. I have a supply of the stuff at home. It was not generally a big deal to see blood.

Until now.

Now, the sight of her bloody finger did something to me that concerned me greatly. It stirred a hunger in me. Real hunger. My stomach growled and my mouth watered and I hated myself all over again. I forced myself to look away, gritting my teeth and grinding my jaw. I looked down at my own pale hands and was surprised to see I had balled them into fists. Purple veins crisscrossed just below the surface of my skin.

A bleeding finger should not arouse a hunger. A bleeding finger should not arouse a *need*. It was just a wound.

Unless, of course, you were a fiend.

My stomach growled and roiled. It seemed to turn in on itself. Jesus, my sudden hunger was unbearable, unrelenting.

"Jesus," I whispered, still looking down at my clenched fists.

"Are you okay?" asked Allison. She was standing nearby. I could hear her sucking on her finger now.

My stomach nearly did a somersault.

Jesus.

I looked up, despite knowing that doing so might be a mistake. It was. Allison was still alternately sucking her finger and looking at the wound—and wincing. I didn't wince. I stared. No doubt hungrily.

It's just a wound, a voice in my head said. The voice, I knew, was the last vestiges of my humanity. *Just a wound. An injured finger. Nothing more, nothing less.*

Except I knew that it was more. So much more. The wound, and the resultant blood, represented so much. It represented complete satiation. Unlimited life. Unlimited strength. Complete and utter superiority.

I blinked. Hard.

Since when did superiority matter to me? Since when did I ever care to be better than others, or control them?

I didn't know, but that train of thought alarmed me more than my hunger. That train of thought was dangerous. Violent. Scary as shit.

"Oh, does blood make you queasy?" asked Allison.

I blinked and might have nodded.

She went on, moving her hand out of my line of sight. I tracked her finger closely, the way a cheetah might a wounded warthog. "I'm sorry," she said. "I was cutting an apple when the phone rang. My mom. Always my mom. Especially with Caesar gone. Everyone calls me these days. Everyone feels sorry for me. Anyway, long story short, I cut my finger pretty deep."

"I see that," I said, the words coming out sounding guttural, and not my own. "And, yes, I have a...problem with blood."

"Oh, geez. I'm sorry," she said sympathetically enough, but she was looking at me oddly. I didn't blame her. I suspected I looked like a complete freak, staring pale-faced, my voice barely intelligible.

Samantha Moon, ace detective at your service.

She went to the bathroom and returned with a Band-Aid. She was watching me as she returned. I knew she was watching me, but I ignored her curious stare. Instead, I was openly staring at her finger like the hobgoblin that I am.

"I'm just going to put this Band-Aid on. Do you want me to do it in the other room?"

"No, here is fine," I said, perhaps a little too quickly. I leaned forward a little in the process to get a better view of her finger.

God, help me, I thought.

Allison continued watching me as she sat across from me on the coffee table. She was Hispanic. Very toned. Lean muscles undulated with each movement. She was wearing short white shorts and a tight tank top. She looked, if anything, like the girlfriend of a world-class boxer. I knew from Romero that she was a personal trainer and competitive body builder. I didn't doubt it.

Except I wasn't looking at the way her muscles rippled or flexed. I was closely watching the way she removed the Band-Aid from the wrapper. She next peeled away the protective backings, exposing the sticky underside. I noted the way her blood continued to fill the open wound. It really was a nasty cut.

I began sweating.

What the devil was wrong with me? But I suspected I knew. I hadn't had human blood in a few weeks, and I was missing it terribly. I didn't want to miss it. In fact, I had made it a point not to think about it.

But to see it now...right in front of me...triggered something in me that I was having a terrible time controlling. Or dealing with.

I looked away, breathing hard.

"Boy, you really do have a problem with blood," said Allison.

I think I nodded. Who knows. Maybe I drooled like ghoul. I kept looking away, breathing slowly through my nose, focusing on the thing that was in front of me, which was a magazine with Katie Holmes on the cover. She looked happy and unencumbered. The words above her said: "Freedom."

"I can go in the bathroom if you want," said Allison.

I was about to tell her to please do so, but there was something in her tone. Something...challenging.

"No, don't," I said. "I'm okay."

"You don't look okay."

"I've been...sick," I said, using my old standby excuse.

"I'm sure you have," she said, her words surprising me. "I'm sure you've been very, very sick."

I looked at her sharply. She had quit playing with the Band-Aid, which now dangled from her finger and thumb. She was squinting her eyes a little. Squinting them at me.

"You're here to find out who killed my Caesar," she said. She lowered her wounded hand in front of me.

"Yes," I said. The word was barely understandable to my own ears. The significant wound along her finger had begun bubbling over again with fresh hemoglobin.

"You are here to help us find answers," she said.

I nodded again, this time unable to speak.

"And you're also a vampire," she said.

I looked at her sharply, and her eyes narrowed further still. I said nothing. She said nothing. Blood was now dribbling freely down her finger. I swallowed hard. It was all I could do to not lunge forward and seize her finger.

She leaned toward me and held her finger in front of me. Like a carrot. "And you're very, very hungry, aren't you?"

I flicked my gaze from her wound to her eyes and found myself nodding.

"Then drink, Samantha Moon."

25.

It was after.

I hadn't drank much, but it was enough to feel good. *No, great.* To feel that special surge of energy, strength and vitality gained only by drinking human blood. *Fresh* human blood.

And never had the blood been as fresh as this.

It was straight from the source, so to speak.

I had also drank enough to be embarrassed, especially now as I sat back on the couch and wiped my mouth. I looked away.

Had I really just drank from her? From her finger? Sucking on it like a newborn from a teat?

I had...and I had loved every second, even when she looked away, clearly uncomfortable and perhaps even in pain. Still I drank from the open wound in her finger. I drank and I drank.

It wasn't until when I had stopped, until when I removed my lips from around her finger, when my eyes finally focused again, did the embarrassment set in.

Allison had immediately pulled her hand into herself, holding it close to her side, as if she were cradling a baby chick. And that's how we currently sat. She, sitting on the coffee table, holding her hand. Me, on the couch, embarrassed as hell and slightly confused over what had just happened.

Lord, I don't even know her.

"I'm...sorry," I said after a moment or two. Outside, through the open sliding glass door, laughter reached us from the street below. Car doors shut firmly, and I suspected one of the limos had just left the scene.

"For what, Samantha?" asked Allison. She seemed to recover from whatever it was she'd gone through. She looked at her finger. "For being what you are? And for that, there is no apology needed."

"How—" But my words stopped abruptly when I looked at her finger. The wound was gone.

She saw the surprise on my face. "Yes, Samantha. Your healing qualities extend to your victims." She turned her face toward me...and smiled deeply. "Even willing victims. It's why, I suspect, vampires have existed among us for so long. The victims' wounds almost always heal."

I opened my mouth to speak, but I still hadn't completely regained my voice and, quite frankly, I felt a little high. The fresh blood was intoxicating, to say the least.

Her blood, I thought. *I drank her blood.*

"How...how do you..."

"How do I know so much about vampires?" she asked, finishing the sentence for me. "How do I know so much about your kind?"

"Yes," I said finally.

I quickly got over the initial high—the contentment, the satiation—and focused on my surroundings. After all, it's not every day that someone so easily surmised my true nature. So then what the hell was going on here? Was this some kind of a set up?

I doubted it.

For one, my inner alarm hadn't sounded. Two, I had sensed nothing but mild curiosity radiating from Allison. Nothing hidden. Nothing darker. Nothing malicious. But I'd been wrong before.

Finally, she said, "I was a plaything to a vampire, Sam. There's no easy way to say it. He used me, abused, me, and drank from me."

"He?"

She smiled again, and now I did sense something else coming from her. Waves of sadness. "He's dead now, killed by a vampire hunter who very nearly killed me, too."

She reached for a packet of cigarettes that were on a shelf under the glass coffee table. She opened the box and tapped out a cigarette and offered me one. I took it without thinking as she produced a lighter from a pocket and we both lit up, exhaling together.

"I'm sorry," I said.

She shrugged and dragged deeply on her cigarette. "I loved him, but he was a bastard. I suppose he had it coming to him."

I didn't know what to say, and so I smoked quietly, which was something I actually enjoyed doing. The act was very human, very real, and had no ill effects to my body, which was a plus.

She flicked her gaze my way. She studied me for a beat or two. "He also got that very same look in his eye. The one you had earlier. When he was hungry. Or when he saw blood."

"What look?" I asked.

"It's a fire. I can see it. Not everyone can see it, but I can."

I saw it, too, but said nothing. After all, I had seen it in Hanner's eyes last month. The smoldering fire. Just behind her pupils.

"Your eyes actually lit up. Fired up. Literally." She laughed. "You were either a vampire...or one sick chick."

I laughed, too. Nervously. All of this talk made me feel uncomfortable. After all, I was discussing my closely guarded secrets with a complete stranger. Then again, I had drank from her, hadn't I? Didn't that make her a kind of blood sister?

God, my life is weird.

As we finished our cigarettes—along with two more—she told me her story. She had met the vampire at a nightclub, where she'd been a go-go dancer. She had always been attracted to bad boys. He was the baddest of bad boys. She could see it in his eyes. He was trouble. He was dangerous, and he was a killer. She sensed all this from him. She had always sensed things from people, her whole life. Her grandmother had always told her she was a sensitive.

Later, after a night of dancing, he had brought her home and made love to her, unlike any man she had ever been with before. His home had been in the Hollywood Hills, and there she learned just how deep pleasures could go. He next fed from her. Without asking. Without prompting or warning. He began drinking from her forearm. She had fought him at first, until she realized the feeling was...incredible.

"Incredible?" I said.

"Don't you know, Sam? May I call you Sam?"

"I just drank from you," I said. "You can call me whatever you want."

She laughed a little. "The pleasure I receive from a feasting is almost as much as you receive from the feeding."

I hadn't known this.

She nodded. "You must be new to all of this."

"Fairly," I said, and left it at that.

She nodded after a moment. "I get it. You don't want to talk about it. It's personal shit. Trust me, I know. Nothing more personal than being what you are." She snubbed out her third cigarette. "I was addicted from the get-go. Addicted to being feasted upon. To being drank from. To being sucked. I was his for as long as he wanted me. Turned out, it was only for a few months."

"Until he ended up dead."

Her eyes filled with tears. "Right, dead. The bastard broke into the house. Shot my man in his sleep. In his *sleep*."

"I'm sorry," I said again.

She shrugged again, something I was beginning to think she did a lot. "Well, like I said, my vampire was a bastard. According to the hunter, my guy had hurt many people."

Now she was silent for a long time. I could hear her heart beating, which surprised me. I wondered if it had to do with me drinking her blood. Maybe we really were blood sisters.

Finally, she looked sideways at me, and put on what I suspected was a brave smile. "But that's not why you're here, Sam. Is it? We're looking for another killer."

I nodded, briefly jolted back to the reality of the situation. "Yes," I said.

"That's good," she said. "Because I have a theory about Caesar's death."

"A theory?"

"Yes," she said. "And you're going to think I'm crazy."

She looked at me. I looked at her. And we both laughed. "Well," she added, "crazier than you already think I am."

I laughed again, and by the time she was done telling me her theory, I decided that she was right.

She was crazy.

26.

She and Caesar had been at a charity event six weeks ago, exactly two weeks before his death.

Caesar was always doing charity work for the Latino community, and this event had been no different. Well, except for one small occurrence, an occurrence that Allison didn't think was small at all. It was an occurrence, in fact, that she was quite certain had been very big indeed.

So big that it killed Caesar.

Or so she felt.

It had been a charity fight. A professional boxer against a martial artist. And he was not just any martial artist: the current, reigning karate champion. The match had gone well enough for the first few rounds. Lots of posing and light punches. Lots of ducking and juking and sliding and laughing. Good times. The crowd was loving it. And why wouldn't they? Two pros at the top of their respective worlds, were matching techniques, wits, and punches.

Until it happened.

The Punch, as Allison thinks of it.

One moment the two fighters were exchanging cushy punches. The karate champion was even doing a few kicks that Caesar easily avoided. After all, this was a charity event. The punches and kicks weren't meant to land. And if they did, there wasn't much force behind them.

Allison had been on the phone, talking to a friend, when the fight suddenly took a very strange turn.

"He punched him, and hard," said Allison now, lighting up another cigarette and sitting back on the couch.

"Who punched whom?" I asked, fairly certain I was using correct English. I was a vampire momma, after all. Not a grammarian. If that was even a word.

"The karate champion," said Allison, exhaling. "One moment they were exchanging light punches —most of which were glancing off each others' shoulders—and the next..." She paused, looked at me. "And the next, this guy, this asshole, punches Caesar hard. I mean, really fucking hard. Caesar wasn't expecting it. It was a charity event, for crissakes. The first few rounds were light and easy. In fact, it was only a three-round charity match. There was only like twenty or so seconds left in the third round. It was almost over."

I perked up. "And this happened two weeks before his death?"

"Yes."

"What happened to Caesar after the punch?"

"It laid him out. Remember, the karate champion was using his *bare fists*. Caesar had gloves on. The fight was just for laughs. A joke. Nothing serious. Just two guys lending their names to a charity event."

I nodded, thinking, mind racing. There was something here. I could feel it. Whether or not this something was my enhanced psychic abilities kicking in or my detective instincts, I didn't know. Sometimes it's impossible to know. Logic suggested that the punch had occurred far too early —two weeks, in fact—for it to have any ill effects on Caesar's health.

And yet...it just felt right.

"How was Caesar after the fight?" I asked.

"Woozy. The punch really rang his bell. Remember, the guy was like a five-time karate champion. The dude knows how to throw a punch. But there's more."

I waited. I considered lighting up another cigarette myself, but didn't want to smell too much like smoke around the kids. Tammy has a sensitive nose, and there was a good chance she was allergic to the smell of cigarettes.

I can't buy a break, I thought.

When Allison had gathered her thoughts, she

said, "I haven't told anyone this, mind you."

"I understand," I said.

"I mean, no one would believe me."

I nodded encouragingly, waited.

"You're the first person who I think I can trust with this information...and perhaps the first person who wouldn't laugh me off immediately. Maybe you are a godsend."

I wondered what God thought of that, but said, "Well, drinking someone's blood has that effect." I didn't mention that she also knew my super-secret identity, which bonded us further. Or condemned her.

She took in some air and plunged forward, "Caesar was never the same after that punch."

"What do you mean?"

"He was different. Not entirely...there. He seemed to have suffered a concussion, of some sort, but the doctors who checked him out said he wasn't showing typical concussion symptoms—nausea, blurred vision, vomiting, stuff like that."

"So what was wrong?"

Allison thought about that, pursuing her lips. "Well, everything, actually. He rarely talked. Rarely slept. I would often find him sitting in the dark alone. He spoke in a monotone. He rarely laughed, and when he did, it seemed forced. My last memories of him are not good ones. My last memories of him—namely the two weeks leading up to his fight in Vegas—were filled with constant worry and concern."

"The doctors couldn't pinpoint anything?"

"The doctor didn't think anything was wrong."

"And you think the punch had something to do with his death?" I asked.

Allison held my gaze. I suddenly felt as if I'd known her for a long time. As if this wasn't our first meeting. I shook off the feeling.

She said, "I know the punch had something to with his death, Sam." She got up and moved over to her sliding glass window and looked down at the street below. "I just know it. And he should never have fought Russell Baker."

"What do you mean?"

"He wasn't ready for the fight. He was still out of it. I mean, Jesus, he was *sleeping* before the fight. Sleeping. He never sleeps before a fight. He was usually bouncing off the walls."

Her words triggered a memory. "Romero told me he had to calm Caesar down before the fight."

"Usually. Romero was always good at getting Caesar to focus, to channel his energy, so to speak."

"But not this last fight?"

"No. Caesar was already calm. So calm that he was sleeping."

I nodded and thought about all of this, and kept thinking about it all the way home.

27.

It was late.

I was at home, looking into Allison's allegations. Unfortunately, there was no video of the charity fight anywhere. That would have been nice to see. The karate champion in question was Andre Fine, and he was generally recognized as the best in his weight class, holding various titles and many degrees of black belt. Apparently, he was the baddest of the bad.

I found his website and studied his many pictures. I also found many YouTube video clips of his fights. He was, from all appearances, lightning fast, and tended to really hurt his opponents. More than one went down and stayed down.

I sat back and rubbed my eyes out of habit.

Truth was, they didn't hurt. Truth was, they never hurt and I had perfect vision. Especially after a day like today.

When I had consumed fresh human blood.

Human blood from a more-than-willing donor.

The small amount that I had indeed consumed from Allison's finger was more than enough to sustain me for a day or two. Human blood has that effect: long-lasting and filling. Even small amounts of the stuff went a long way.

I thought of Allison again, a woman who loved to have her blood consumed. And I mean *loved* to have it consumed. And here I was, a woman and vampire who knew the benefits of human blood. The supernatural, unparalleled benefits. It was hard not to see that this could be a match made in Heaven.

Or, more accurately, in one of the outer rings of Hell.

Andre Fine. He looked like a tough dude. He knew how to punch. How to guard. He seemed to have an almost supernatural grasp of what his opponent would do next. From the footage I saw, no one had gotten close to him. No one had hurt him, and all were beaten—badly.

Except, he didn't strike me as something supernatural. He wasn't a particularly big man, and, according to Kingsley the Buttface, I now knew that werewolves actually grew in size as time went on. Kingsley himself had started out as a much smaller man, which made me wonder how big Kingsley would eventually get. Or, if there was a capping-off of size.

Then again, maybe I didn't care, at least, not about Kingsley.

But I did care. I did care that he had cheated on me, and it was all I could do to not drive over there, kick his door in, and then kick his face in.

But he had been set up.

So what?

Easy excuse.

Jerk off.

Perhaps Andre Fine was a *new* werewolf, then, not yet old enough to achieve the bigger size. Kingsley, after all, possessed such quickness and strength. But Andre Fine was slight, even. He was, in fact, often smaller than his opponents...although clearly faster and stronger and more skilled.

I shifted gears, and within a few minutes, I had all his personal information in front of me, as well. I now knew his last three residences, including his current one in Malibu. He was single, no kids, and had an interesting rap sheet. He'd spent time in county jail for beating a man nearly to death in a barroom brawl. His hands were registered as lethal weapons, so the fight was considered a felony. He also seemed to like to beat up his various girlfriends. Three different complaints from three different women. No arrests, warnings only. I looked up his birth certificate, and confirmed that he was not an immortal who had lived hundreds of years, although he certainly fought like an immortal. He was thirty-four.

Still, how could a single punch have an effect a month later?

I didn't know. But I knew someone who might. I picked up my cell and called Chad Helling, my ex-partner with HUD. He answered on the second ring.

"Better?" he asked.

"I like being a second-ring kind of gal," I said.

"You do realize we're not partners anymore, Moon Shine," he said, using one of his trillions of nicknames he had for me. "I'm not obligated to pick up at all. In fact, my life would be a lot easier if I just let your calls go to voicemail."

"Then why don't you?"

"I said my life would easier."

"So that means you still love me."

"No, I love Monica. I put up with you."

"Good enough," I said.

"So, how can I plunder the government's resources for you this time, Sunshine?"

"Not the government's resources. Your gray matter. I'm calling to pick your brain. I need your expertise."

"In beer?"

"Fighting," I said, knowing that Chad Helling was an amateur MMA fighter.

"Sometimes they're one and the same," he said.

I rolled my eyes. I told him about my case and about Allison's theory. And to my complete surprise, Chad didn't laugh immediately, which is what I had expected.

When I finished, he said, "Andre Fine is a bad dude."

"That's what I gathered."

"No, I mean a bad dude."

"Okay, you lost me," I said.

"I mean, the guy is legendary in the fighting community. Not only is he the reigning karate champion, but he has been for the last five years in a row."

"But why is he legendary?"

"Did you catch the part about being champion for five straight years?"

"I did," I said. "But I also noted something else in your voice."

"Geez, Moon River, I can't keep anything from you."

"Nope. Now, out with it."

"Okay, here's the dope."

"Dope?"

"It's like the new catch phrase these days."

"Fine. Give me the dope."

"Ugh."

"Ugh what?" I said.

"Doesn't sound right coming from you. Sounds too mom-ish."

"Well, I am a mom. Now tell me what you know or I'll shove my mommy sneaker up your ass."

"Now that's the Samantha Moon that I remember."

"Chad..."

"Right. Fine. Look, some of this isn't easy to talk about. I mean, it's kind of crazy, actually."

"Crazy, how?"

"You know about Bruce Lee, right?"

"Sure," I said. "Kung fu guy?"

"Well, he was much more than just a kung fu guy, but yeah, him. Anyway, he died of cerebral edema caused by pain medication. A bad reaction, you know? He died at age thirty-two."

"So what about him?" I asked.

"In 1985, *Black Belt Magazine* stirred up some controversy when it suggested that Bruce Lee had, in fact, been killed by a *dim mak*."

"*Dim mak*?"

"Death touch."

"Of course," I said.

"You might laugh but there are lots of fighters and martial artists out there who think the *dim mak* is real."

"And how might one die from a *dim mak*?"

"That part isn't so easy to explain. But it has something to do with stopping life flow or life force, or what some call *prana*."

"Did you just say *prana*?"

"I know. New Age-y, woo-woo stuff. But think of it as the opposite of acupuncture, which encourages the flow of energy through a body."

"And the *dim mak* discourages the flow of energy?"

"That's the theory."

"On Google, do I just type in *death touch*? Or

touch of death?"

"Like I said, Moon Glow, you can laugh, but there are many who believe it's real—and a few who claim they've seen the *dim mak* in action. And those who are reputed to have the skill are given a wide berth."

"Let me guess..." I said.

I could almost see Chad nodding his squarish head over there on his side of the line. "Yes," he said. "Andre Fine is one of those who's reputed to know the *dim mak*."

"Lucky him," I said.

28.

I was sitting at my desk, drumming my fingers, listening to my children sleeping from down the hallway, thinking about damned "touches of death" when it happened.

It was a vision.

A powerful vision, so powerful that I knew it could have only come from Fang. It filled my waking thoughts completely, blurring my vision enough for me to believe that what was happening to *him* was happening to *me*.

This happened to us sometimes. If Fang was experiencing something powerful enough, emotional enough, or exciting enough, it nearly always flooded my thoughts.

As it did now.

Usually, I can switch off the image, and leave Fang to his privacy. But as I sat back in my desk chair, the image I saw in my mind made me gasp.

It was of Detective Hanner. And she was hovering over Fang, straddling him. She was wearing next to nothing. The light shifted. His eyes shifted. Correction. She was, in fact, wearing nothing. Standing over him, naked.

I shouldn't be watching this, I thought.

I could turn off the image. Block it, so to speak.

But I didn't. I continued watching, like a voyeur through a bedroom window. I watched because I suspected I knew what was going to happen. I knew it, but I wanted to be sure. I wanted to see it for myself.

Fang, I saw, was naked, too. He was sitting in a chair. I could see his chest heaving. His skin was gleaming slightly. I hadn't seen him naked before. This was a first... and it was impressive. All of it... and all of him.

But I was seeing what he was seeing, and now his gaze shifted as she slowly swung a leg over him and straddled him. I felt him shiver. Heard him moan and gasp. She adjusted herself on him, reaching down, and now he moaned low and long as she slid him inside her.

A powerful wave of pleasure swept through him and subsequently me, too. I felt him throbbing.

Jesus, no wonder guys love those things so much.

But this wasn't about sex. I knew that. Fang

knew it, too. This was just preparing him for what was to come. He was waiting for it. I could sense his thoughts, even if they were a bit scrambled. He was willing her to do it, to do it, to do it.

Please. Do it. Please. God, please.

His thoughts briefly overcame mine, his line of thinking replacing mine.

I shook my head, and nearly pulled out of the scene, but I had to see what happened next. I had to see what was going to happen to my one-time friend, Fang.

Do it, love. Do it, baby. Do it, do it. DO IT!!

I shook my head, trying to clear it, trying to focus on what was happening, but Fang's thoughts were too intense, too powerful, too overwhelming. I had two choices only: block the vision completely... or give into it.

I debated only briefly.

And gave into it...

29.

They writhed.

I writhed, too, along with Fang, since I was living through him, experiencing through him, feeling through him. All while I sat here alone in my office, while he made love in another part of town, with a vampire.

A very dangerous vampire.

I did not feel jealous. I loved Fang, but for different reasons. He had been a friend first...and a stalker later. Knowing his past later did not wipe away the feelings of warmth I had developed for him. He had helped me through some very dark times in my life, and for that, I would always be grateful.

That he had had an agenda only came out later.

Agenda or not, he had always been my Fang, my friend, my confidant, my rock, my source of information and sometimes, even inspiration.

But I was losing him tonight.

I was losing him forever.

The sound of his panting filled my thoughts. I could also feel his heart racing. Nearly uncontrollably. Fang had the mother of all delusions. Early on in life, thanks to a rare defect, he had believed he was a vampire. And a part of me suspected he *still* believed he was a vampire.

At least, a vampire at heart.

Fang was the embodiment of the Law of Attraction. He believed it hard enough, wanted it bad enough, lived it, breathed it...and now he was about to become it.

The real deal.

A vampire.

His lifelong wish, his fondest desire, his burning passion was about to become real, and he could barely control himself. No, he couldn't control himself. I felt ghost tears pouring down my face. But they were his tears pouring steadily down his face. Our connection was still so strong, so powerful. In this moment, we were one.

I could stop the connection, but still I resisted.

I had to know what was happening to my friend... I had to know what was going through him, and what she would do to him.

She writhed on his lap, faster and faster. From his blurred vision, I saw his hand reaching up for her hair, pulling on it. She went with it and bared her teeth. Not unnaturally long canines, no. Normal teeth. I was the same. My teeth were always the same size. Nothing pointy. Nothing I ever had to hide.

Thank God. Going through this life was hard enough being what I was. At least I didn't want to have to keep my lips closed, too.

Her teeth were unnaturally white. Same with mine. No coffee stains. No yellowing. Apparently, a steady diet of blood whitened teeth, too. Go figure.

Her chest was small. Not a lot of bouncing or heaving there, but I saw that one of Fang's hands were groping them absently. Mostly he was concentrating on her face, her mouth. I saw what he saw—and he was laser-focused on her teeth.

Her pure white teeth, which she flashed once more.

She was going to do it. She's doing it. Please do it. Please. I need this. I have to have this. I must have this.

Fang's vision focused and unfocused, wavered, spun briefly. He was close to hyperventilating. Close to passing out. He wanted this so bad, was so excited, so turned on...

Deep breaths, Aaron, he told himself, his thoughts appearing in mine. *Deep breaths. There. There. She's doing it. Oh, God, she's doing it...*

His eyes unfocused and I saw that Hanner had indeed lowered her face...briefly to his lips, which she grazed with her own, now down along his chain and onto his neck, all of which she kissed and licked hungrily...

Jesus, it's really happening.

I wasn't sure if that had been Fang's thoughts or my own, until I realized it didn't matter.

One thing I did know was that Fang was close to orgasm.

Jesus, I shouldn't be seeing this, feeling this, I thought.

Her rhythm increased, her hips riding me—Fang—harder and faster. I felt her body thrust against me, her breasts grazing me. Her lips kissing me. Fang and I were one, truly one, and it was all I could do to not gasp. Something was rising in him, an incredible sensation. It was building powerfully. He gripped the chair he was sitting in. I gripped my own chair.

And just as I felt a sharp pain in my neck—no, an excruciating pain—Fang released powerfully into her, crying out, holding her tightly.

Even while she drank deeply from him.

30.

It was the next day, and I was with my daughter.

We were at the Brea Mall, which was next door to the same Embassy Suites where I had stayed for a few weeks last year, back when my ex-husband, Danny, had been trying to destroy me. He's cute like that.

I was holding Tammy's hand. These past few days, ironically, she had seemed inseparable from me. She had only run away for a few hours. It had been just long enough to miss her mommy.

The mall was surprisingly quiet for a Saturday evening, although there was the usual amount of squealing teenage girls. Trailing right behind the squealing girls was a group of giggling boys. This trend was repeated throughout the mall, on every level of every quadrant. From Macy's to Nordstrom's, from Sbarro's Pizza to Wetzel's Pretzels: laughing girls were followed closely by giggling boys.

Of course, there were whole families here, too. And couples shopping, and security guards strolling, and glass elevators elevating, and escalators escalating.

But none were as loud as the squealing girls.

"You don't have a lot of friends," I said after we stopped for pretzels.

I ordered two out of habit. I wasted more money that way, and as we continued our slow stroll through the mall, I broke off a big chunk of pretzel and just held it. I waited until Tammy turned to look at a poster of the latest *Twilight* movie, this one called *Midnight Sun*, and dropped the chunk of pretzel into a trash can. That was a damn shame, since it smelled heavenly and there were hungry folk in the world.

Tammy glanced over at me and smiled. I smiled, too, and pretended to swallow the non-existent pretzel.

I hated my life sometimes.

We continued like this until we got to the downstairs courtyard near JCPenney. When Tammy conveniently turned to look at something that surely caught her eye, I quickly disposed of the last of the pretzel—

But not in time.

She quickly glanced back at me...and only then

did I realize that I'd been set up.

"Mommy?" she said.

"Uh, yes?" I had looked away, feigning interest in some shoes in a nearby window.

"Mommy, why have you been throwing away your pretzel this whole time? I've been watching you do it in all the windows." She looked at her own reflection in the store window and stared at my hand-less sleeves. "Well, sort of watching you."

Caught. Dammit.

"Mommy has a stomach ache," I said.

"But you always have a stomach ache."

"I know, baby. Sometimes Mommy is very sick."

"But you're always sick. If you didn't want the pretzel, then why did you order it?"

"I wanted it, sweetie. Very badly."

She stopped walking and took my forearm. Long ago, she had quit asking me about my cold flesh. Cold flesh and Mommy were one and the same. "Enough double talk, Mom."

"Double talk?"

"Yes. Double talk. It means you are telling me one thing but mean another."

"Oh, it does, does it?"

"Yes, it does. Mrs. Marks explained it to us the other day. And I realize that you do that a lot. Double speak."

"You think so?"

"I know so, Mommy. For instance, if you wanted the pretzel so badly, then why not eat it?

Then why *pretend* to eat it? And if you actually had a stomach ache, then why order it at all?"

I crossed my arms under my chest and leaned a shoulder against the window. I glanced at the time on my cell. He should be here any moment now. For once, I wished that Danny was early.

I said to Tammy, "I don't know, honey. You tell me."

"I think you do know, Mommy. I know lots of things these days."

"What things?" I asked.

"Secrets."

"Whose secrets?"

"Everybody's secrets."

"How do you know their secrets, honey?"

"I see them."

"See them how?"

"I just see them. Like visions."

"I see," I said. "So, what secrets do you know about Mommy?"

"For one, you've been lying to me and Anthony for years."

I opened my mouth to speak but nothing came out. My lips and tongue worked to form words, to no avail. Mercifully, across the mall, Danny appeared through the crowd, looking grim-faced and handsome and moving quickly.

"There's another, slightly bigger secret," she continued, following my gaze and seeing her dad approaching.

"What?" I asked with sickening dread.

"You're a vampire."

I think my eyes just about bugged out of my head, not that I could see my reflection. I pushed off the window just as Danny appeared and hugged Tammy. She hugged him back, but kept her eyes on me.

"Where's Anthony?" he asked me gruffly.

"He's with his cousins this weekend."

"Fine. Tell him I miss him."

"Will do," I said. But I was looking at Tammy.

Danny nodded and was about to turn away with the palm of his hand on Tammy's lower back, when he suddenly stopped. He looked at me curiously, then his daughter. "Everything okay here?" he asked.

"I don't know," said Tammy, "Ask Mommy."

"Yes," I said. "Everything's fine."

"Fine, whatever," said Danny, and now he took Tammy's hand and led her off for his weekly visitation.

As she followed behind him, Tammy looked back once...and gave me a knowing smile.

31.

I was sitting in my minivan, admittedly shock-ed.

My innocent children were innocent no more. Gone were the days where they would blindly accept Mommy's complaints of a tummy ache or of a rare skin disease or my even vaguer explanation that "Mommy is just cold."

I started and tried to predict the significance of Tammy also knowing that her mother was the freak of all freaks. I wondered if there was any hope that my kids might still might grow up to be normal...and that thought alone nearly overwhelmed me. I buried my face in my hands all over again. I sat like that until the tears stopped.

As I sat there, face in my hands, two things

occurred to me: one, how deep my hate was for the angel, Ishmael; and, two, that my daughter was steadily growing more psychic.

And when, exactly, did that happen?

I didn't know or had been too busy to notice. And where did these gifts come from? I didn't know that either. My son's own great strength was far easier to explain away. That his sister would also have abilities was beyond me.

As I contemplated this, drying my eyes, a sudden and severe pain blasted through me, doubling me over, wracking my body. I doubled over, and knew immediately the source of the pain.

Fang.

Still doubled over in the driver's seat, hands gripping the steering wheel, I shielded my thoughts, throwing up a mental wall around me. Immediately, the pain subsided, and then passed completely. But I knew the pain.

Intimately.

I had gone through it myself seven years ago, after my own attack. Fang was going through what I now knew was the transformation from mortal.

To immortal.

And I knew he was alone in his apartment, and scared shitless. I felt his fear, along with his pain. I took in a lot of air, drummed my fingers briefly on the steering wheel, and then headed out of the parking lot.

To Fang's apartment.

32.

Fang.

My best friend. Perhaps even more than a friend. My mentor. His advice had been crucial. His guidance had been invaluable. It was safe to say that I might have—just might have—gone batshit crazy without his help.

No pun intended.

That he had stalked me and fallen in love with me were different matters entirely. That he had been a friend when I needed a friend the most was what I would always remember.

I was sitting across from him now in his small, one-bedroom apartment located at the edge of Fullerton, in a shabby complex where the great Philip K. Dick had once lived. Fang was lying on his couch in the fetal position, shaking violently. I was certain that he was not aware of me.

I was certain, in fact, that he was dying.

According to Fang, this was the very complex where Dick—the author of *Blade Runner* , *Total Recall,* and *Minority Report*, to name a few of his more popular titles—had his reality-shattering religious and visionary experiences.

Except now, as I watched Fang curl tighter into the fetal position, I knew there was nothing religious or visionary going on here. What I was seeing was a man suffering horribly.

I knew the feeling; it wasn't nice.

What was going on here, I knew, was death. His body wasn't just changing into something out-of-this world. It was dying, pure and simple. And Fang wasn't just dying, I knew. He was being...

Replaced.

Something else would inhabit him. Something dark and sinister—and looking for a foothold into this world.

Jesus.

The energy around Fang was interesting, to say the least. The deep black halo that surrounded him was infused with particles of light. I had never seen that before. I was witnessing something extraordinary.

I had only been to Fang's apartment once, months ago. Back then, I was still on the fence with Fang, still open to the possibility of romance. He had served drinks and we had sat on this very same couch. He had played music and I knew his intention was to seduce me. There were some benefits to reading the guy's thoughts, after all. But we never got very far. From the moment he put his arm around me, I had known that this was wrong. I had stood and told him that I was sorry but I had to leave.

Fang had looked mortally wounded, but had given me a sweet kiss on the cheek and told me to drive safely.

And now I was back, and watching him writhe and sweat and pant on the couch. That is, until I heard the sound at the door.

Detective Hanner of the Fullerton Police Department was standing in the entrance, watching me carefully. How she got in without me hearing her was disturbing. We stared at each other some more. My shoulders tensed. I was ready to move quickly if I had to.

But I didn't have to. She nodded to me after a moment, then turned and quietly shut the door. Once done, she tossed her coat over the back of a dining chair and walked toward me. Her eyes didn't exactly glow, not like Kingsley's, but I could see what appeared to be tiny flickers of flames just behind her pupils.

"Good evening, Samantha Moon," she said evenly. When she spoke to me alone, she always spoke differently, reverting to a slightly formal way of speech, tinged with a hint of an Eastern European accent. Perhaps it was her natural dialect from wherever it was she hailed.

My inner alarm began ringing. I watched her carefully, aware that there was also movement in the shadows to my right. The movement, I knew, was not from a physical form. Something had, I was certain, materialized *within* the shadows. A shadow within a shadow. My alarm grew louder. Now I saw it from the corner of my eye, creeping away from the far wall.

A living shadow.

Hanner, as far as I could tell, was unaware of the shadow. Or chose not to acknowledge it. "I would strongly advise you, sister," she said, "that you not disrupt the *changing.*"

Outside of a creepy book that had once called out to me, I had never been referred to as sister before. I didn't like it. It made my skin crawl. It made me feel less than human.

More than human, hissed a voice in my head. *Always more than human.*

And now I did turn—in time to see something step away from the wall. No, *peel away* from the wall like a pitch-black sticker. Although still dark as night, the two-dimensional shadow fleshed out, so to speak, into something three-dimensional, into something with depth and substance.

The entity soon stood before me, in the center of Fang's living room, rising and falling gently on ethereal tides that I neither felt nor saw. It was tall, a foot or so taller than me. But narrow. Its shoulders were nearly non-existent. Shadowy hands ended in curved, shadowy claws that opened and closed below its narrow hips. It stopped before me and I knew it was regarding me.

You spoke to me, I thought.

Yesss, the entity hissed, and I saw that its head tilted slightly to one side. Black mist swirled around it, rising up from Fang's carpet. *You are a sssister of the night, Sssamantha Moon. You would do well to never forget that.*

I knew that most supernatural entities did not have access to my thoughts, unless said entity was old enough or powerful enough, as was the case with Captain Jack last year.

And now, of course, this entity.

Can she see you? I asked it, indicating Hanner in my mind.

The entity paused only briefly before words appeared in my thoughts. *No, child. Only you can.*

Why?

There was another pause, this one much longer. *That remains to be ssseen.*

What do you mean? I asked. I sensed the thing before me was eager to move forward, to join its new host.

You are very, very sssensitive, Sssamantha Moon. Yesss, I am eager to claim my host.

I had another psychic hit, one that came to me with crystal clarity. *You have been dead a long time.*

The creature rose and fell silently. *A very long time, Sssamantha Moon. Too long.*

But you were once alive, I thought, as the hits continued. *Once human.*

Very astute, child. And now I will be alive again. Just as my sssister is alive again in you.

But why? I thought. *I don't understand.*

It isss the way, came the reply. *The only way.*

With that, the shadow slipped past me. Hanner was stroking Fang's hair, unaware of the approaching shadow behind her.

"No!" I shouted.

But as I spoke those words and as Hanner whipped her head up to look at me, the shadow poured forth into Fang, into the region of his heart. Fang gasped, his chest arched up. His eyelids fluttered wildly, and the dark halo I had seen around him, the halo once speckled with light, winked out of existence.

And with it, something else.

Fang's presence in my mind.

He was gone.

Forever.

33.

Fang settled back down onto the couch. The shaking, I noted, had stopped. His panting, too, stopped.

I suspected, on some level, that his body had expired...that it was now being fueled supernaturally by the dark entity that had entered him. I also suspected his soul was now trapped in this supernaturally vivified body. Forever.

"His mortality ends," said Hanner next to me. "And his immortality begins. Everyone should be so lucky."

Fang was closed off to me. Our connection was forever severed. I had mixed feelings about that. My connection to Fang had been turbulent, at best. At times, it had been comforting. To know that I had instant access to someone who seemed to legitimately care for me—and perhaps even love me in his own way—was a rock I had relied on for many months now.

Except that Fang always had an ulterior motive. Considering how the man had grown up and issues he'd dealt with, his ulterior motive would surprise no one. That he stalked and befriended and ultimately loved a real vampire should be of no surprise either.

I had seen more than enough of Fang's mind to know the man was single-mindedly obsessed. His desire to be a real vampire trumped anything, perhaps even his love for me.

As I looked at him now, lying there quietly, I noted that the wound in his neck—the wound I, myself, had felt just the night before—had already healed.

Yes, his desire to be a vampire had trumped even his love for me.

"Why did you do it?" I said to Hanner, without looking at her.

"I saw his potential, Samantha."

"He's not stable," I said.

"I'm not looking for stability. I'm looking for potential."

I nodded, understanding. "His potential to kill."

"So much potential."

"That's why you turned him," I said, looking at her. "To kill for you."

She calmly looked up from Fang and at me. She

held my gaze. The fire just behind her pupil flared brightly. "He is his own free man, Samantha. But I am sure he will show his appreciation when I am done revealing to him all that I know."

"You're doing this because I shut down your operation," I said. "You're punishing me. You're stealing my friend—"

"I'm giving him everything you wouldn't, Samantha."

"You'll create a killer."

"He will be tamed, Sam. Even the worst of our kind can be tamed."

"Or what?"

"Or they are removed."

"You mean killed."

"You cannot kill what's already dead, Sam. The entity within will simply withdraw, sacrificing its existence for the betterment of our kind."

"And when the entity withdraws?"

"The body will perish. Instantly."

"Jesus."

Hanner winced slightly at my involuntary utterance, which I noted. The name "Jesus" had no effect on me, but it appeared to on Hanner.

Interesting, I thought.

"And what happens to his soul?" I asked.

"His soul?" asked Hanner, looking at me and making an almost comical effort to blink. "But whatever do you mean?"

"His soul," I said, my voice rising. "Where is it?"

Hanner smiled and it was, perhaps, the most unpleasant smile I had ever seen on anyone. *Ever.* "Why, Samantha. His soul is long gone."

A wave of panic swept over me. I wrapped an arm around myself. Hanner's unpleasant smile remained frozen on her face. The smile was not human. She did not look human. She looked slightly misshapen, hunched. She looked like pure evil.

"You're not Hanner," I said. "You're the thing that lives in her."

"Very good, Samantha Moon," she said. Or *it* said.

"And you're trying to freak me out."

Hanner continued smiling that wicked smile. Or the thing within her did. "Is it working, child?"

"Go to hell," I said.

"Been there, done that," it said in a monotone, tilting its head slightly.

"Where's Hanner?"

"She's here. Next to me. Waiting. I've come for the big show."

"Big show?"

Hanner nodded toward Fang, who lay motionless on the couch. "I wouldn't miss his transformation for the world."

"Who's in me?" I asked.

Hanner grinned, except I knew it was not Hanner grinning. "One of us, child."

"Who?"

But Hanner shook her head. "Not now. Not now." And Hanner kept on shaking her head...and finally blinked. Hard.

She was back, looking slightly confused, and the thing within her—the thing that galvanized her dead body—had retreated, and was gone.

That such an entity was in me, watching over me, living through me, was almost enough to drive me insane.

Almost.

There had to be a way to fight back. To remove it.

And with that thought, I remembered the angel, Ishmael. He had told me he knew of a way for me to be free, to forever remove the thing within me. I thought about that, even while Fang continued to lay motionless, his chest unmoving. But alive. Supernaturally alive.

Fang had gotten his wish.

He was one of us now.

34.

I was flying.

It's what I did these days when I want to think —and apparently, I was one of the few who could.

Lucky me.

I was moving along the beaches, idly following the curving shore. It was hours before morning, hours before I would be exhausted enough to sleep...but not so exhausted that I had to sleep. The medallion had removed the effects of sunlight, but not my natural—or *un*natural—sleep patterns. My body still craved sleep during the day, happily doing so until sunrise if I would let it. Two kids and a full-time job, unfortunately, wouldn't.

I flew five hundred feet above the crashing surf. The beaches were empty. Correction...mostly empty. There was a lone man jogging with a little squirt of a dog. A little red dog. Yes, my eyes are that good at night and in this form. The man looked vaguely familiar. Tall and muscular. As I flew overhead, the little dog stopped and barked. At me. The little shit. The man, stopped, too, and looked up, but I was already gone. I smiled to myself, now recognizing the cocky son-of-a-bitch.

The ocean rippled and sparkled, reflecting whatever ambient light was around. Fang would never be the same. Our relationship would never be the same. Hanner had plans for him, I was sure. But she could shove her plans up her pale ass.

We'd see about her plans.

Was Fang's and mine a true friendship? Perhaps, perhaps not. I liked to believe it was. I liked to believe he cared for me beyond what I was.

I had not yet made a decision about what to do about Fang's request. Truth be known, I was afraid of what would happen once I did. I was afraid for our relationship, for him, for the world. Of course, Detective Hanner had made the decision for me, thus forcing mine and Fang's relationship to make that leap.

Fang was no puppet. Hanner was in for a surprise. Unless, somehow, the two of them had made a pact. Perhaps he had sold his soul, so to speak, to become that which he most wanted. Perhaps I had doomed him by delaying my own decision. Perhaps had I honored his request, he would not be bound to Hanner.

Was Hanner so bad? I didn't know. Not yet.

But one thing was sure: I would be there for Fang, for whatever reason, at any time. He had been there for me...and I suspected he was going to need my help.

Or perhaps not.

After all, he had Hanner now.

With a heavy heart, I turned to starboard, dipping one wing and raising the other, and headed over the million-dollar homes and back toward Fullerton.

35.

I was familiar with boxing gyms; not so much with dojos.

Andre Fine's Kenpo Karate Studio in Long Beach was about what I expected to see: lots of floor mats, lots of mirrors, two punching bags, a trophy case and tons of newspaper and magazine clippings adorning the entrance/lobby room. A schedule next to the door indicated the next class would start in two hours.

Presently, there wasn't a soul around. I heard someone talking in a back office. On the phone, if I had to guess. Single voice speaking, pausing, then speaking, then yelling. More yelling. Then a slam.

Oh, goodie, I thought. *At least they'll be in a good mood.*

A man appeared a moment later, dressed in jeans and a t-shirt. He had a small beer gut and thick arms and a lot of muscle around his shoulders and neck. Probably, when he was in uniform and wore a karate robe, it bulged and opened around his mid-section. He probably *hee-yahed!* with the best of them. And I had no doubt that he had punched his way through many a wooden board in his time.

The man, who might have been talking to himself—and not very kindly—looked startled when he saw me. "Can I help you?"

"I'm here to see Andre Fine," I said, reaching in my purse and extracting a business card. I held it out to him. "I'd like to ask him a few questions regarding a case I'm working on."

He took the card, read it, and then handed it back. Most people don't hand my cards back. Most people hold them politely and talk to me civilly—then throw them away as soon as I leave. Handing my card back irritated me. Handing my card back made me hate his face. Handing my card back stirred a surprising amount of anger in me.

Down girl, I thought.

The anger subsided enough for me to reach out and take the card back and not break his fingers in the process. And as I took the card and slipped it back in my purse from whence it came, I had an image of me slamming this stranger up against the trophy case and...

Drinking from his neck.

Jesus.

This wasn't a normal reaction from me. This wasn't how I handled animosity. Not with anger. Not with violence. Maybe with a cute quip. Or to just brush it off. Not with images of violence.

It's him, I thought suddenly. *It's his thoughts. His anger. His violence. The thing inside me.*

"Hey, you okay?" asked the guy. To his credit, he looked a little nervous.

He should be nervous.

Again, that wasn't my thought. I wiped the sweat from my brow and nodded. "Yeah, I'm fine. Is Andre around?"

The guy looked at me some more, then got around to my question. "Sorry, but Andre doesn't actually work here. Sure, his name is on the sign outside and all the letterheads, but the truth is, he rarely shows up anymore. I thought you might want your card back because I would hate for you to waste it on me when he's never around."

I paused and collected my thoughts. "Thank you. Where...where can I find him?"

"These days? Pick any one of his many girlfriends. Sorry, I shouldn't say that about my boss, but he's a hard one to pin down lately."

"Why's that?"

"Hard to say. Too many distractions maybe. Too much success. Too many endorsements. Too many women."

"What would he say if he heard you say that?"

"I don't know. And I don't really care. This place is going to hell in a hand basket and he doesn't care. I just got off the phone with another parent who's pulling her kid. I don't blame her. It's hard to pitch a world-class studio when the head guy rarely, if ever, makes an appearance."

"Is it common for karate champions to own a studio?"

"Common and expected. And the ones who do at least make a courtesy appearance every now and then to keep everyone happy, maybe a demonstration here and there, something to keep the customers coming back."

"I've heard rumors that Andre Fine has been trained in," I paused, picking my words carefully, "other areas of martial arts."

The big guy crossed his hairy arms. "Oh? In what other areas of martial arts?"

I sensed that he knew immediately where I was going with this. I sensed that I wasn't the only one who had asked him this question. I also sensed that such accusations had been whispered about Andre Fine for many years now. But these were much more than just feelings. I had slipped briefly into the big guy's thoughts. I had done so effortlessly. All I had needed were a few moments with him. Now we were connected mentally. Only, he didn't know it.

"What do you know about *dim mak*?" I asked suddenly. "Or the *touch of death* as some call it?"

He chuckled lightly and blew air through his flat nose, air which ruffled his thick mustache. He waved his hand dismissively. "*Dim mak* is a bunch of hooey."

His thoughts gave him away. He didn't want to talk about it. In fact, he very much wanted me to leave and was thinking hard of an excuse to give me.

No excuses, I thought. I hadn't planned on directing his thoughts. I hadn't planned on anything of the sort when I arrived here just a few minutes earlier.

But seeing the direction he was going with his thoughts, sensing his intention to mislead and misdirect me, I instinctively stepped forward. I had not been aware that I could direct another's thought until speaking with Hanner last month—and watching her manipulate a theater of police officers.

I had thought I would never do it.

I had thought I would never resort to controlling another human being's thoughts.

But something within me *wanted* to control his thoughts. *Needed* to control him. *Needed* him to do my bidding. I suspected I knew what this something was.

I didn't want to control him. All I wanted was the truth. I wanted to know what he knew about Andre Fine. It was as simple as that.

Tell me what you know about dim mak, I thought.

He glanced at me, and as he did so I saw something disconcerting. His expression went blank. Dead. He opened his mouth to speak, faltered, then tried again. "*Dim mak* is not very well understood." He spoke in a flat monotone. "But it is real."

"Has Andre Fine been taught the *dim mak*?"

"Oh, yes. He's spent many years in Japan learning it from those who specialize in it."

"And what does the *dim mak* do?"

"It kills if struck correctly."

"And you believe this?"

"I have seen this."

"You have seen Andre Fine perform it?"

"No, another."

"And what was the result?"

He looked blankly. "Death."

"How long ago did this happen?"

"When I was in my twenties. I was a new fighter. We had all heard rumors that it was going to be performed in a fight."

"Tell me about the fight."

He did, speaking in his dead monotone. The fight had been an arranged fight. Both fighters were highly accomplished, and both were reputed to have mastered *dim mak*. The fight had occurred in a field, well away from the city. The fight itself had been a fairly long one, with both fighters evenly matched. That is, until one fighter struck the death blow. The *dim mak*.

"And what happened after that?"

The guy licked his lips and said, "The other fighter went down."

"Was he alive?"

"Yes."

"When did he die?"

"Two weeks later."

"And you believe it was because of the *dim mak*?"

He looked at me...and smiled emptily. "I know it was because of the *dim mak*."

Later, as I drove home, I realized that I hadn't even gotten the guy's name. I had controlled his thoughts, made him do my bidding, and I didn't even have the decency to know his name. Seemed rude.

Yeah, I thought. *I'm a monster.*

36.

"Well?" said Tammy.

We were in her bedroom. Anthony was in his room playing something called Nintendo 3DS. Whatever it was, it was little and expensive and if he ever lost it, I was going to play butt bongos on his backside until the cows came home. And since there weren't any cows in Fullerton, that might be a while.

"Well what?" I said. We were sitting on her floor in the space between her bed and dresser. Her back was to me and I was brushing her long hair.

"You know, Mom. Don't play cloy."

"Coy," I said.

She sighed. "Whatever, Mom. Cloy, coy. Either way, out with it."

"Since when did you get so demanding?"

"Since I realized that my mother has been lying to me my whole life."

"Not your whole life," I said, doing some quick math. She would have been about three when I was attacked. Anthony had been one. I had been a relatively new mom with one really freaky secret.

"So you've been lying for part of my life?"

"And since when did you get so smart?" I asked. She was skewering my words like an attorney. Like father, like daughter. That is, if you could call an ambulance chaser an attorney.

She waited, and not patiently. Down the hall, I heard Anthony groan and slap the floor, which sent minor shockwaves throughout the whole house.

He's getting stronger, I thought.

"I will tell you...more about me," I said. "But first, I want you to tell me why you think I have such a big...secret."

She held up her forefinger. "First, I don't think you have a secret. I know you have a secret." She raised another finger. "Two, you've always been weird."

"Thanks," I said.

"I mean, a person who can't go outside in the sunlight? A rare skin disease? I mean, c'mon!" She raised a third finger, and a fourth and fifth as she ticked off more points. "Three, you're always cold. Four, we have like *no* mirrors in the house. Five, you never eat." She lowered her hand and spun to face me. "Oh, you *pretend* to eat, but lately I've

167

been secretly watching you sneak your food onto Anthony's plate. He's so dumb. He never notices it and just eats it. Such a doofus."

"Don't call your brother names."

"Sorry."

"Apology accepted," I said. "So tell me when you started having, you know, visions. When did they start?"

"Last month."

"When your period started," I said, nodding.

"Mom!"

Tammy hated talking about it, true. She thought it was gross, try as I might to convince her that it was the most natural thing in the world. Still, at ten, she was young to have started her period. She was young, but it was not unheard of. I had been ten, too, when mine started. Like mother, like daughter.

"Anyway," she said, rolling her eyes, "when *that* started, I also started seeing things."

"Seeing what?"

"I started seeing thoughts, I guess."

"Your own thoughts?"

"No, Mom," she said, nearly rolling her eyes full circle. "*Other* people's thoughts. I can already see my own thoughts. Duh."

"Be nice."

"Sorry."

"So, what did other people's thoughts look like, honey?" I asked.

She looked away, bit her lip. The aura around her was a light blue. Peaceful blue. There were flashes of greens and yellows, but she often had flashes of greens and yellows. Some colors were simply a part of someone. These were her colors. And, as always, I had no access to her thoughts. Other people's, sometimes. My own children, no.

Finally, she said, "They sort of appear as pictures. Fast pictures. They come and go quickly."

"How do you know they are not your own thoughts, honey?"

"Because they are things that I have never seen before. Things I had never *thought* about. Things I wouldn't..." She struggled for the right words.

"Things you wouldn't know," I offered.

"Yes, Mommy."

"So what did you think when you saw these strange images?"

She shrugged and reached down and cracked one of her excessively long toes. I cringed. I hated the sound, and asked her to stop. She rolled her eyes.

"Well, I was confused. But then I saw that the images seemed to come from people around me. I would see, for instance, Anthony's teacher in class, but from Anthony's eyes."

"So you concluded you were seeing his memories."

"Yes, Mommy."

"And the images only came to you when other people were nearby?"

"Yes!" she said excitedly. I think she figured I wouldn't believe her. Or that she was doing something wrong, somehow.

"So you weren't hearing their thoughts," I said. "But rather *seeing* their memories?"

She nodded and reached down for her toes, but then thought better of it. "I think so, yeah. Take Ricky Carpettle—he's the kid who always has boogers stuck to his forehead, 'cause, you know, he wipes his nose *up* instead of down. Anyway, I kept seeing him playing video games in his Batman underwear."

Despite myself, I laughed. I said, "How often do you see these images?"

"As often as I want."

"How do you stop them?" I asked.

She thought about that. "Well, I just sort of say 'Stop!' in my head real loud, and the images, you know, go away. At least, for a little while."

We were both silent. My daughter was a friggin' mind reader. How this came to be, I didn't know. Did her abilities have anything to do with me being a vampire? If so, how? My attack seven years ago should have no bearing on who or what she would become later in life.

My head hurt...briefly. I never had headaches for long. Still, I rubbed my temples, thinking hard. When I was done rubbing, I saw that Tammy was watching me closely. I didn't have to be a mind reader to know what she was going to say next.

"And when I'm around you, Mommy, I see things, too."

"Oh, God."

"You can fly, Mommy."

"Oh, God," I said again.

"It's you. I know it. But it's not you. You are something else, something huge. With wings, and you fly high above."

And now I really did have a headache, one that lasted a few seconds longer than normal. I buried my face in my hands and rubbed my head and wondered why the Universe was determined to utterly ruin my life and those of my kids.

"It's true, isn't it, Mommy? You can fly."

And the words I spoke next to my daughter should have sent me straight into an institution. Straight into a straitjacket. To be locked up forever. Words no sane person should ever, ever have to say. Especially not a mother to her daughter. And yet I heard them come from my mouth. I heard them from a distance. I heard the insanity of it all.

"Yes," I said, my face still buried in my hands. "I can fly."

37.

"What are you guys talking about in here?" asked Anthony, sticking his head in the doorway. I'd heard him coming and kept my face buried in my hands.

"About adult things, butthead," said Tammy angrily. "Now go away."

"You're the butthead. You go away."

"He can stay," I said. "And you both just lost TV and video games for the night."

"Can I still play computer games?" asked Anthony.

"Aren't those the same as video games?"

"No, Mom. Duh."

"Then those, too," I said. "And no one goes on the internet, either. Oh, and both of you hand over your phones."

They did so grudgingly. We had a fairly wide-ranging Netflix account. Apparently, anything with a screen these days could access the TV. I thought of anything else I might have missed, going down my mental checklist: TV, Xbox, phones, computers, laptops. I snapped my fingers.

"Leave your iPads in my office, too."

"But Mom!" they both said in unison.

"That's what happens when you call each other names. We're a family. We don't call each other names."

"Since when?" asked Tammy.

"Since forever. And especially now. If you want to question me further, young lady, you can see what life is like without a DVR player."

"Sheesh. Sorry."

"That's better. iPads. Office. *Now*."

They stormed off. Tammy grabbed her iPad from her desk. I heard Anthony rummaging around his room for his own. I silently longed for the days when no TV had been enough. I also silently longed for the days when I could eat heaps of guacamole and chips. They returned a few moments later, both looking glum.

"Anthony, come in and shut the door. I'm going to talk to both of you."

Anthony's eyes widened a little. After all, he had done a darn good job of concealing our secret from his sister, although I suspected, with her newfound gifts, his secret wouldn't be concealed for long.

Too many secrets, for too long.

I patted the carpet in front of me and told them to sit. They sat. It was time for the truth, and so, I reached out and took their hands and told them everything. From my attack seven years ago, to my ability to fly, to their father's revulsion for me, to Kingsley Fulcrum being just as much a weirdo as me.

I told them everything.

Everything.

38.

We were at Cold Stone Creamery.

"Isn't it nice to know that you don't have to keep faking it all the time, Mom," said Tammy as we all sat in a booth in the far corner.

Although the weather was warming, the creamery was empty. I wasn't complaining. My kids couldn't keep their voices down even if I paid them to. Especially not now. Not with this much excitement in the air. After our talk a few hours ago, it had been Anthony who suggested we all go get ice cream. No surprise there. The kid was literally eating me out of house and home.

Interestingly, just in the past two hours, the kids were getting along better. And not just getting along but being—and get this—*friendly* toward each other. At one point, Anthony suggested to Tammy that she try the Snickers on her ice cream, and she actually did. She didn't tell him to mind his own business. She didn't ignore him. She didn't tell him he was stupid and looked funny. She said, "Sure."

I stood there in amazement, watching the scene play out. Tammy then nudged Anthony and pointed to a big stain on the worker's apron and they both giggled.

Together.

Granted, they were laughing at someone else, but at least they were getting along.

Baby steps.

I considered Tammy's question as I sat with the two of them. I was drinking from a water bottle and chewing gum. The gum was nice. It only gave me the smallest of stomach cramps—no doubt from the trace ingredients in the flavor—but it was nice to chew and drink and look like a real mom. I said to Tammy, "Yes. It is a relief, actually."

"You don't have to keep pretending to eat or to have stomach aches," said Anthony.

"At least, not around you two," I said.

"Or Daddy," said Anthony.

"I don't eat with Daddy anymore."

"Oh, right."

Tammy was eating her ice cream thoughtfully. "But when we are around other people..."

"Yes, I will still have to pretend to eat, or pretend that I'm full, or pretend that I have a tummy ache."

She nodded thoughtfully. Somewhere through all of this, my daughter had seriously grown up. Having access to others' minds might have something to do with that. Or maybe it was realizing that her mother was the mother of all freaks, too.

"Remember, what I am," I said to them again, "is a secret."

"We knoooooow," said Anthony, laying his head on the table. "You told us like a Brazilian times."

"Bazillion," Tammy corrected. "Brazil is a state."

"Country," I said.

"Whatever," she said. "The point is, we all have secrets now. We should make a pact."

"What's a pact?" asked Anthony.

I waited for his sister to ridicule his question, or, at least, to roll her eyes at his simplicity. She didn't. Instead, she surprised me again by turning to him and saying patiently, "It means we all agree to something forever."

"Forever?" said Anthony, blinking. "But mom's a mimmortal."

"Immortal," said Tammy, only slightly losing her patience.

"That's what I said. Mimmortal. She lives forever. That's a long time to keep a secret."

I nearly fell out of my seat. Listening to my kids discussing something so casually that I had tried so hard to keep secret from them was just too surreal. I didn't know if I should smile, weep, or fear for the mental health of all of us.

"Okay," I said. "We'll make a pact to keep our secrets forever. Deal?"

"Deal," they said together.

We all looked at each. Anthony voiced what was on all of our minds. "So, how do we make a pact?"

"I honestly don't know," I said.

"A blood pact!" said Tammy.

"I don't wanna make a blood pact!" screamed Anthony.

"No blood pacts," I said, shushing them. The Cold Stone worker had looked over at us.

"How about an ice cream pact!" said Anthony, although I was pretty sure no one knew what he was talking about, least of all himself.

I said, "How about a pinkie pact."

"Yes! A pinkie pact," shouted Anthony.

Tammy nodded, too, and we all held our pinkies over the slightly sticky table. We interlocked them. Theirs were warm. Mine, not so much.

"Pinkie swear," I said.

"Pinkie swear," they said together.

"To keep our secrets to ourselves."

They both nodded solemnly, and we unhooked our pinkies and Anthony was about to go back to his ice cream when he paused and said, "Tammy can really read my thoughts?"

"Yup," she said.

"That is so weird."

"No weirder than you being half vampire."

"I'm not half vampire. I'm just strong like a vampire. Like Mom."

"That's the half part, buttface."

"You're the buttface, buttface."

"You can't say buttface twice, buttface."

"You just did!"

I rolled my eyes and checked my watch. They had gotten along for all of two hours.

Better than nothing.

39.

The Pacific Ocean at sunset.

It was beautiful. Expansive. Tinged with so much color that one's soul sang. Even souls trapped in immortal bodies.

As I drove north along the Pacific Coast Highway toward Malibu, I realized that today was the first day that Kingsley had not tried to call me or text me. I had always kept Kingsley at arm's length. I had done so for a number of reasons, and one of them was because I suspected he would do something like this. The man was an infamous womanizer.

Maybe I had been too cautious with him. Maybe I had shut him out of my heart for too long. Maybe I had made it easy for him to be with another woman.

To fuck another woman.

I was pressing hard on the gas again, too hard. I was whipping past other cars at an alarming rate. I eased up and unclenched my grip on the steering wheel.

According to Kingsley, he had been ready for a relationship. He had been ready to settle down, to explore something serious. I hadn't been. I was dealing with a lot of hurt and had no business starting anything new with Kingsley. But he had been persistent, and sexy as hell...and unlike anything I had seen before.

But a tiger didn't change his stripes.

Granted, this tiger—or wolf—had a little help from above. Namely from my guardian angel who had set Kingsley up. And Kingsley, being the dog that he was, fell for it hook, line and sinker.

Bastard.

Maybe I should thank Ishmael for showing me Kingsley's true colors. Then again, maybe I should tell Ishmael to go to hell, since he'd caused this mess in the first place.

But didn't he give you immortality? a voice inside me asked. *And the gift of flight? And great strength?*

Had that been me asking those questions, or the thing inside me? I didn't know. Still, they were valid questions.

So I thought about them as I drove on. Ishmael had acted out of love and selfishness. Tainted love. Ishmael had put me in unparalleled danger. He had risked my life...

He had risked his own salvation for love. His love for me.

He had risked everything.

For me.

I thought about that...and I continued thinking about that even as I pulled up to Andre Fine's Malibu beach home.

40.

The house was gated and beautiful.

It was also difficult to find for anyone who wasn't an ace private investigator. Andre Fine wasn't showing up in my basic records searches. No surprise there. Many celebrity-types were hard to find. Often their properties and homes were in the names of their accountants or managers or other family members. In Andre Fine's case, the home was under a sister's name. It was a nice precaution to keep people like me from looking them up.

Except most private investigators didn't have the federal government's massive resources at their disposal. Or an ex-partner who owed his love life to them.

I wasn't here to interview Andre Fine. I wasn't

here hoping he would see me. I suspected there was one way—and one way only—to get a confession from him.

For now, I waited down the street in my minivan, where I hoped to attract little or no attention. Generally, a woman sitting alone in a minivan on a quiet street attracted little attention. A man in a minivan would warrant a call to the police.

Sometimes it's good to be me.

Or a woman.

As I waited and watched, I reflected on the fact that tonight was a big night in the Moon household. After all, tonight was the first night that Tammy and Anthony would watch themselves. Without a babysitter.

Tammy was proving to be surprisingly mature, and Anthony was already stronger than most men. My sister, of course, was on high alert, with her phone nearby. Forty minutes into my surveillance, my text message alert chimed.

I glanced at the phone, my heart immediately racing. Was there something wrong at home? If so, why would they text and not call? I grabbed my cell and swiped it on.

A single message from Tammy: *Ant's being a jerk.*

I frowned and dashed off a text: *Don't call him Ant. You know he doesn't like that. And kindly turn your TV off for one hour.*

But why? she wrote back almost instantaneously.

For calling your brother a jerk.

But Mom!!

Another text came through, this one from Anthony's cell phone: *Fanny's being mean.*

Don't call your sister Fanny. No TV for the two of you tonight.

Not fair!

You're mean.

This sucks.

Anthony's feet smell.

Tammy's breath smells. So do her armpits.

My armpits do not smell. I'm a girl!

How I got into their loop of name calling, I didn't know. But they continued like this for the next few minutes...all while I shook my head sadly. Finally, I put a quick call in for my sister, who told me she was on her way over. I checked the time. My kids had watched themselves for all of two hours.

Again, better than nothing.

***

An hour later, a convertible BMW with its top down came up behind me. It was silver and sleek and probably more expensive than my house in Fullerton. Seated in the driver's seat was none other than Andre Fine. A beautiful blond was in the passenger's seat next to him. Both were laughing as they drove past me. Neither glanced at me. Just another perfect day in Malibu.

He turned into his driveway, waited a moment for his electric fence to swing open, then continued on, disappearing behind a long row of thick hedges.

I waited another half hour, then stepped out of my minivan.

41.

The gate was six feet high, made of wrought iron that was curled into vines that culminated into spikes.

As far as I was aware, there weren't any security cameras. And if there were, I wasn't worried. Since I wasn't wearing make-up tonight, anyone reviewing the footage would seriously question their sanity, or the equipment. They would see moving clothing, and not much else.

Yup, I'm a weirdo.

I glanced up and down the street, saw that I was alone, gripped one of the iron spikes, and jumped. I was up and over in a single leap, landing lightly on the other side.

There were no guard dogs, although a fat white

cat skittered off past the BMW and clawed its way over a side fence. I decided to follow, this time hurdling the side gate in a single bound, no hands needed. I cleared it by a foot or two, and marveled again at my own athletic prowess. I wondered how I would fare in the Olympics.

Maybe Michael Phelps was really a vampire.

Or a mer-man.

Once in the backyard and away from prying eyes, I scanned the side of the house, looking for my opening. No, I wasn't against breaking a window or smashing through a door, but if there was another opening, I would take it.

The house was Spanish colonial and epic. The plastered walls were smooth and tan, and I was beginning to wonder just how much a karate champion made. There, on the third floor, was a wide veranda with an open French door.

I gauged the jump...and realized it might be too high for even me. Thirty feet was pushing the limits of what I could do until I spotted a drainage pipe snaking down near the balcony.

Good enough.

I gathered myself, took a breath or two, then leaped as I high as I could. At just over twenty feet up, I grabbed the drainage pipe and used it to catapult myself the remaining ten feet, where I cleared the balcony railing and landed smoothly on the deck.

The balcony reminded me of a particular crime lord's balcony out in Orange County. Same beautiful construction. Stone columns. Marble railings. Epic view of the Pacific Ocean. At the time, the crime lord's night had not gone very well. In fact, he'd ended up dead. We'd see how Andre Fine would fare.

There was a sound behind me. A woman's voice. Humming.

I turned in time to see the same blond woman I had seen in the passenger seat emerge from the bathroom. She was fully naked and surgically enhanced. She was working a towel through her wet hair when she saw me. Her mouth opened to scream.

I was moving. Fast.

Just as a strangled cry escaped her lips, my hand clamped around her mouth. My other hand grabbed her around her waist and now, I was dragging her quickly across the polished wooden floor and into a walk-in closet. I threw her inside and shut the door, but before I did, I saw way too much jiggling.

Far, far too much.

There was a heavy, antique dresser along the nearby wall, and I wasted no time putting a shoulder into it. Heavy was right. It took me a few seconds to move it into place in front of the closet, cleanly knocking off the door handle in the process.

The woman inside found her lungs and let loose with the mother of all wails. Andre Fine, looking cut and chiseled and very fine himself, emerged out of the bathroom with a toothbrush dripping from his mouth.

"Jill?" he mumbled around the brush.

"She's presently indisposed," I said, "but still very jiggly, which, I'm sure, is how you like her."

He spun at the sound of my voice, the toothbrush flung out of his mouth, splattering foam across the wooden floor. He ignored the toothbrush. I figured I would, too. Instead, he stared at me and was no doubt doing his best to process what he was seeing. Instead of his bodacious and very naked girlfriend, he was looking at a spunky, dark-haired vampire with lots of attitude.

His eyes next went from me to his freshly relocated dresser now standing guard in front of his closet, a closet from which muffled cries and screams and banging could be heard. Andre Fine's face went through a number of emotions then, the most prevalent being disbelief and shock.

I get that a lot these days.

Andre was a tad under six feet but held himself well. Like a fighter. He balanced easily on the balls of his feet. His body was extremely muscular. His six-pack undulated with each breath. His aura was a vibrant green, flashing with wild energy around him. The faster the energy, the more likely he was to spring into action. More muffled shouts came from the closet.

"What's going on?" he said.

"We're going to talk," I said.

He scanned the room, tilting his head a little, listening hard. He was someone who trusted his senses, his instincts. I could see that. That was probably why he was such a good fighter. Except now the information that was being returned to him had to be a tad confusing. A woman alone. A house broken into. His jiggly girlfriend was imprisoned in a closet, a closet which was now barred by his heavy dresser.

"Who's here with you?" he asked.

"Just little ole me."

Without taking his eyes off me, he nodded toward the blocked closet. "Who moved that dresser?"

"That would be me."

He stared at me for another two seconds. "I'm calling the police," he decided.

"No, you're not."

"Do you have a gun?"

"No."

This time he actually shook his head, no doubt trying to clear it. "How did you get in?"

I grinned and pointed at the balcony. I grinned because his robe had fallen open and I could see his wahoo. Not very impressive. Then again, I had been dating the hulking Kingsley.

"Your weiner's showing," I said.

He ignored me. "Why are you here? What do you want?"

"We're going to talk about Caesar Marquez. And you're going to put your little wee-wee away."

He did so, absently, tying off his robe.

"You're here alone?" he said, clearly confused by this notion.

"Yes."

"Do you have any idea who I am?"

"Yes. You're Andre Fine. Five-time karate champion and, according to some, an expert at *dim mak*. Or the touch of death."

He shook his head some more and walked out into the middle of his room. He turned and faced me. "And you broke into my house?"

"Technically, I didn't break anything. Think of it more as *appeared*. I appeared in your house."

"You have a lot of balls."

"I have a lot of something."

He stared some more and the energy around him crackled, picking up. His bright green aura turned brighter. Added to the mix were some hot pinks and reds.

"Who do you work for?" he asked.

I shook my head and walked toward him. "New rule. I ask the questions from now on."

He watched me closely, eyes narrowing. He was also slowly getting into a fighter's stance, perhaps unconsciously. Jill screamed again from inside the closet, banging against the sturdy door.

I stopped a few feet from him. "You're confused as hell, aren't you? Poor guy. A woman comes here. Rearranges the place. Makes your big-boobed girlfriend disappear. Stands here alone, unarmed and unafraid. Confusing as hell, I imagine."

His eyes continued to narrow, even as he continued lowering into a fighting stance.

"Makes you want to do what you do best, huh?" I said. "To fight?"

He'd had enough. He lashed out with a straight punch that was much faster than I had anticipated.

42.

But he wasn't fast enough.

I tilted my head to the right just as his punch *whooshed* past my ear. His hand snapped back immediately and he looked at me comically, blinking rapidly. He hadn't expected to miss. He had expected, no doubt, to knock me out cold.

A woman. Nice guy.

He stepped back, cracked his neck a little and did a little dance to loosen up his limbs. His little pecker poked out again, curious.

I didn't move. I didn't answer. I didn't get into a fighter's stance. I said, "During an exhibition fight two weeks before Caesar Marquez's death in the ring, you delivered what many thought was a cheap shot."

Andre said nothing. With his aura crackling a neon green, he lashed out again. This time I didn't bother moving my head; instead, I brushed off the punch with a swipe of my hand. My counter-block had been fast. Supernaturally fast, and it sent Andre's forward momentum off to the side, where he stumbled a little, but quickly regained his balance.

"It was supposed to be an exhibition," I said, watching him. "I called the event organizers. No live punches. Just light stuff. Easy-to-block stuff. Entertain the crowd. Great photo ops. Three rounds of laughter and fun and good times."

Andre was bouncing on his feet now, bouncing and kind of circling me, too. There was no confusion on his face. Just grim determination. I had seen the same look in many of his YouTube videos. He was treating me like an opponent. I felt honored.

"But in the last twenty seconds of the third round, you punched Caesar Marquez. Hard. For no apparent reason, and against protocol. Some called it a cheap shot. I call it something else."

Andre Fine turned into a cornered wild cat, unleashing a ferocious onslaught of kicks and punches and spinning jumps, lashing out with elbows and knees and fists and feet. It was a pretty display. I had seen him unleash similar onslaughts against his opponents during his many filmed matches. During those matches, one or more of the punches or kicks would land home, sending his opponent to the mat, and making a winner out of Andre Fine. A five-time champion, in fact.

But here in the spacious area between the foot of his bed and his adjoining bathroom, the area where his big dresser had sat but was now conveniently moved across the room, I blocked punch after punch, kick after kick. Sometimes, I didn't block, but simply moved my head a fraction of an inch. At one point he tried a helluva fancy kick, jack-knifing his body splendidly, swinging his foot around so fast that, had I been mortal, I was certain my jaw would have been broken. I wasn't mortal though, so I saw the kick coming a mile away. Instead, I caught his ankle and spun him around like a ballerina.

We did this dance a few more minutes until I finally found the opening I was looking for, and delivered a straight punch. Nothing fancy. Just a straight shot delivered from shoulder height, and hard enough to send him stumbling backwards where he collided into his footboard, which he held onto briefly, before sinking down to the floor.

I walked over to him, knelt down, lifted his chin with my finger and said, "Now, we're going to talk."

43.

We were sitting on his balcony.

Jiggly Jill was long gone. It turned out that Jill wasn't much of a girlfriend. She had been someone he'd picked up tonight at a party. I doubted she would go to the police. Truth was, she hadn't a clue what had happened to her or what was going on, and just before she left, just as she was pulling on her clothes, I gave her a very strong suggestion to *not* go to the police.

She merely nodded, grabbed her stuff, gave Andre one last, fearful look, and headed out front to wait for her taxi.

"Don't look so sad," I said. "There's more where she came from."

Andre was presently pressing a bag of frozen

peas to his right eye and alternately smoking. It was multi-tasking at its best. I suspected the cigarette might be accelerating the rate at which the bag of peas was melting, but decided to keep my hypothesis to myself.

When we listened to a car door open and heard what we both assumed was the taxi speeding off, Andre ground out his cigarette and looked at me.

"Who the fuck are you?"

"A private investigator."

He blinked. "You're kidding."

"Nope."

"Where did you learn to fight like that?"

I shook my head and motioned to the pack of cigarettes. He reached down and shook one out for me. I plucked it out deftly. He next offered me a light and I leaned into it and inhaled. I exhaled a churning plume of blue-gray smoke, and said, "If I told you, I would have to kill you."

"Fine," he said. "I've never come across someone like you."

"And I doubt you ever will again."

He studied with his free eye; the other being, of course, hidden behind a melting bag of Green Giant peas. "I believe it."

I had a thought, and wondered just how far I could go with this mind-control business. I waited until he caught my eye with his one good eye, and said, "I will tell you what I am, but when I leave your house, you will forget it completely. Understood?"

He looked at me—and looked at me some more —and finally, his one good eye went blank. He nodded. My suggestion had sunk home. A moment later, the dazed look disappeared, and he looked at me again as he had a moment or two before: with confusion and maybe a little awe.

"I'm not human," I said. "Not really. I'm something else. Some call me a vampire."

He lowered the bag of peas. His other eye was nearly swollen shut. I saw it working behind all the puffy folds, trying to see through. "You're serious?"

"Deadly."

"And that explains why you're so fast?"

"Yes."

"And strong?"

"Yes."

He had witnessed my skills firsthand, had seen me doing things he had never seen another human do. It wasn't hard for him to accept that I was perhaps something different.

"But I thought vampires were, you know, only in books."

"A form of them are, yes."

He was about to ask me another question and I shook my head. "We're not here about me, Andre. Do you understand?"

He nodded again, resigned. He returned the peas to his swollen eye and sat back a little in his chair.

I said, "When did you learn the *dim mak*?"

"Years ago. From a master in Japan."

"Have you used it before?"

He brought his cigarette to his lips. "Can't vampires read minds or something?"

"Often."

"So it would do me little good to lie."

"Little good."

"And what will you do with this information?"

"I haven't decided yet."

"Will you go to the police?"

"Maybe. But I doubt they'll believe me."

He chuckled lightly. "True."

Andre Fine was thirty-six years old and well spoken, but I sensed an urban roll to his words. No surprise there, since he had grown up in New Jersey. I knew he had a long list of priors, some of them violent. He had spent six years of his life in various prisons. He was a street fighter—no doubt, a natural fighter—one who had honed his skill into something deadly.

As I sat there looking at him, I suddenly knew why he did what he did. And how he could afford such a lifestyle. Whether it was a psychic hit or not, I didn't know. But I suddenly knew the truth.

"You're a hired killer," I said.

He glanced at me and shook his head and smiled. "You're good, lady."

I waited. He waited. I knew his every instinct was rebelling against talking to me, but I knew he would, even without my prodding.

"Yes, I am. Of sorts."

"What does that mean?"

"It means I can't always guarantee death. Some

survive the *dim mak*." He shrugged. "Others don't."

"Caesar Marquez was one of those who didn't."

He shrugged again. The sign of a true killer. Nonchalance about life and death. Would I ever be that way? God, I hoped not.

"So, people hire you to kill people?" I asked.

"That's how it works, lady."

"Only you can't guarantee death."

He nodded. "It's impossible to guarantee death."

"The victim dies two weeks later," I said, "so no one expects foul play."

He grinned at me, his cigarette dangling from his lower lip. "That's the beauty of it, lady."

"Your hands are registered as lethal weapons, are they not?"

"They are. So, you're really a vampire?"

"I really am."

"Jesus."

"He's not a vampire, as far as I'm aware. Give me your hands."

He did, hesitantly, setting aside the peas. I wasn't compelling him to do what I wanted, but I think he thought I was, and that was good enough. I took his hands and instantly had image after image of bar fights and street fights and back alley brawls. In all of them, Andre was wearing a hood and shades. In disguise.

"So, you often pick fights with your unsuspecting victims."

He shrugged. I'd seen the *dim mak* being delivered, a ferocious blow that left his opponents reeling and dazed.

"You've killed dozens of people," I said.

He shrugged again. "Who's keeping track?"

I stared at him, unblinking. He looked back at me, and promptly blinked and looked away. I sensed his fear, I also sensed he was about to do something stupid.

I said, "Who hired you to kill Caesar Marquez?"

He shook his head. "Sorry, babe. That's where my cooperation ends, vampire or no vampire."

Except as he spoke the words, I saw a brief flash. An image. It appeared briefly in his thoughts and was gone. I released his hands and he sat back with the bag of peas.

"You can't prove any of this," he said. "No one would believe you."

"True," I said. "They wouldn't believe me, but they would believe you."

He sat there and thought about it and smoked, and high above us, a low cloud briefly obscured the stars. The wind also picked up. Somewhere in the Malibu Hills, a coyote howled.

"No one can know about what I've done," he said.

I said nothing and watched him closely. I was certain I hadn't blinked in many, many minutes. He went on.

"My family is so proud. Everyone is so proud. That feels good. It feels good knowing that I did my family proud. We were so poor. The money was so easy." He was babbling now, and I saw the tears.

"Just one punch and I make thousands, tens of thousands. Sometimes, even more."

I watched and waited, catching a brief glimpse of what he was planning on doing.

"I can't let my family down. I can't. They're so proud."

I said nothing, and watched as Andre Fine, a five-time champion fighter, was reduced to tears and incomprehensible mumbling.

I got up and left him there on the balcony.

44.

It was two days later, and I was back at the gym in downtown Los Angeles.

I watched from the shadows as a cadre of boxers did their best to punch the stuffing out of everything from punching bags to speed bags to padded mitts.

Seated with me was Allison Lopez. I held her hand in a comforting, reassuring way. I didn't worry about my cold flesh, and, indeed, she seemed to revel in it. She wanted to meet me here, a place she always found comforting. Apparently, she loved hearing the sounds of boxing. The scuffing feet, the smell of sweat. It was here, after all, that she had watched Caesar Marquez blossom into a world-class fighter.

Now, we were watching a young flyweight,

smaller than me, even, punching the unholy crap out of his trainer's mitts.

"His own brother," she said again, shaking her head.

"Yes," I said.

"But why?"

I looked at the posters that surrounded the gym. Most were of Caesar Marquez. None, as far as I could tell, were of Romero. "My best guess," I said, "was that he was jealous."

"Romero was an accomplished trainer. He was never a boxer."

"Never a boxer *of note*," I corrected. "His official record was nine wins and twenty-three losses."

She blinked and squeezed my hand. "I had no idea."

"Few did. A very unremarkable career."

"But he was so successful as a trainer."

I shook my head. "He was successful at training his successful brothers. Many of whom have had title shots. And Caesar, according to all reports, was the best of the lot."

"Still, why kill him?"

"Maybe he never expected him to die," I said. "Or he never believed he would die."

"He had to believe that some injury would occur."

I nodded. I assumed so, too.

"But how did he know to hire Andre Fine?"

A good question. Two days ago, after meeting

with Andre Fine, I had spent the morning doing some investigating. A quick call to Caesar's promoter, Harry, confirmed that Romero had arranged for the exhibition against Andre Fine. This had surprised Harry, as Romero was rarely involved in fight promotions, or even publicity events. And what Harry told me next surprised me, although it shouldn't have: Andre Fine had once been an up-and-coming boxer, until he turned to martial arts.

"Let me guess," I had said to Harry over the phone. "Romero had been his trainer."

"Bingo," said Harry.

I had next called Allison Lopez and asked her the one question that I knew would break this case wide open. She confirmed my suspicions, and a few hours later, I was at the LAPD in downtown Los Angeles, meeting with a homicide investigator named Sanchez. Sanchez was a big guy with wide shoulders, who sported pictures of his UCLA football days on his desk. His desk also sported pictures of a very lovely wife.

Sanchez listened to my story, listened to the wild tales of *dim mak* and of hired killers and touches of death. To his credit, he didn't laugh or joke or even crack a smile. I told him of Romero's connection to Andre Fine, of Romero setting up the exhibition, and who had benefited the most from Caesar's death. Romero. Romero also happened to be the beneficiary of his brother's life insurance.

Detective Sanchez listened to all of this, then told me he would get back to me.

And he did, a few hours later. They had sent a squad car out to Andre Fine's residence in Malibu, where they had found his body swinging from a rope off his third-story balcony. All indications suggested a suicide. I tried to feign shock and horror at hearing this news, but in truth, I had seen it coming.

They next picked up Romero for questioning. To his credit, he admitted to almost everything. Apparently, Romero was looking to get out of the family business. And he also confessed that he planned to fly the coop, all the way to Bermuda.

Now, I caught Allison up on my investigation.

She said, "God, I remember now. Romero practically forced Caesar to do the fight. He claimed it was great exposure and publicity. Caesar didn't want to do it but his brother reminded him it was for charity and finally, Caesar gave in." She shook her head. "Jesus, set up by his own brother. What a bastard. I fucking hate him."

We were quiet. The gym wasn't. It was a cacophony of grunts and thumps and pounding. It sounded sexier than it was.

"Has the insurance money been awarded to Romero?" asked Allison.

I shook my head. "Not yet. These things take some time on the insurance company's part."

"And now?" she said.

"He paid to have his brother attacked. That will nullify the life insurance policy."

"So, what will happen to Romero now?" she

asked.

"He'll be charged for soliciting Andre Fine to hurt his brother. There's no way a murder charge will stick, not with something like *dim mak*."

"Maybe he never meant for his brother to die," she said.

"Maybe," I said. "But he was willing to take that chance."

Allison nodded. "His brothers won't look kindly on what he did," she said.

"I don't expect they will," I said. "I have no doubt that Romero's life will be a living hell from this moment on."

She nodded and squeezed my hand and rested her head on my shoulder, and, as she wept silently, I watched two young fighters in the center practice ring exchange a flurry of punches. Both were wearing padded helmets. Both were sweating profusely. More importantly, one of them was bleeding from his lip.

I was dismayed to discover that it was the blood, above all else, that interested me the most.

45.

On Wednesday evening at 6:30, Russell Baker and I were jogging at Huntington Beach.

He was shirtless and jaw-droppingly sexy, and it was all I could do not to stare at him as we spoke. Staring at him while we spoke might have led to me running into a trash can. Still, I stole glances, every chance I had. I wondered if it was unethical to lust after my client.

"That's a wild story, Samantha Moon," he said. He always sounded so damn polite when he spoke to me. Too polite. I wanted him to sound...interested. This surprised the hell out of me. A few weeks ago, when he'd first appeared at my house, I had not thought of him as anything other than a client. But watching his fights, watching his skills, seeing the compassion in his heart, and his surprisingly peaceful aura for a fighter, well, something shifted.

That, and the fact that Kingsley had broken my heart all over again.

"It's more than a theory," I said.

"How can you be so sure, Samantha?" he said easily, smoothly, confidently.

"Call me Sam," I said.

"Sure thing, Sam," he said and looked at me and winked and something inside me did a sort of flip. My stomach? Or, perhaps, something further down?

I considered how much to tell Russell, and decided to keep things fairly sanitized for now. "Romero hired Andre Fine to deliver the *dim mak* to his brother."

"The *dim mak*," said Russell, shaking his head, "is only a myth."

"Myth or not, Caesar Marquez died two weeks later during your match, from no apparent punch or series of punches from you. Most people I'd spoken to—from the referee to Jacky—don't think you hit him hard enough to do any real damage."

Russell shook his head. "I'm not sure if I should feel relieved or discouraged."

"It is what it is," I said, hating myself for using such a generic idiom, but I was finding being in Russell's presence, jogging together at the beach, so damn exciting that I wasn't thinking straight anyway.

"I suppose so," said Russell smoothly. "Caesar

was a tough fighter. It was hard to land anything on the guy."

"Could he have been champ?" I asked.

"Maybe," said Russell, and he looked at me and winked again. "'Course, he woulda had to go through me first."

"Of course."

I smiled. He smiled. His stomach muscles undulated. I somehow just missed running into a blue trash can.

Russell said, "You believe there's something to the touch of death?"

"I do."

"Why?"

"The police have gone through Andre Fine's records. There's evidence that he'd been paid for many such hits. For someone who wanted to preserve his legacy in fighting, he sure kept a nice paper trail of his illegal dealings."

"What exactly do you mean by evidence?" asked Russell. He breathed easily, smoothly, his elbows relaxed at his sides.

"Investigators found evidence of nine paid hits, totaling hundreds of thousands of dollars. Seven of the targets are dead."

"Let me guess," said Russell. "They died of unknown brain trauma."

I nodded, although I don't think Russell saw me nod. "Good guess."

"Weird," said Russell.

"Weird is right," I said.

"So, maybe there's something to this *dim mak*."

"Maybe," I said.

Russell looked at me. "Weren't you afraid that he might hurt you?"

"Naw," I said.

"I would have protected you," he said.

And for some reason, that bravado seriously warmed my heart. "That might be the nicest thing anyone's said to me in a while."

He grinned and flashed his perfect teeth. "Except, why do I get the impression you don't need any protecting?"

"Oh, I need *some* protecting," I said.

He slowed down and so did I. He placed his hands on his hips and sucked in some wind, although I got the feeling he wasn't very tired. By my estimate, we had jogged five miles.

"You're not breathing hard," he said.

"Nope."

"You're an interesting chick, Ms. Moon," he said.

"Like I said, call me Sam."

"Would you like to get some dinner, Sam?"

"I thought you would never ask."

46.

The evening was warm and the front door was open.

Outside, children played in the cul-de-sac, laughing and sometimes shouting. I heard the rattle of bikes and skateboards and scooters. Not surprisingly, I didn't hear my own kids.

These days, they stayed in with me. Somehow, some way, we had grown closer, and for that, I was pleasantly surprised. My life had gotten easier, too. Feigning eating or stomach aches and avoiding mirrors had been more stressful than I realized. Now, such worries—at least around my kids—were gone.

Thank God.

Yes, they still had many questions: What did I

eat? How often do I eat? Did I kill people? How strong was I? Could I kick Daddy's ass? Could I fly? And so on.

I answered the ones that were age-appropriate, although I suspected my own daughter could look far deeper into me than anyone else ever could.

Dammit.

No secrets, I thought.

School was nearly out. The kids in the neighborhood were ready for summer. Everyone but my kids were ready. They were, at this very moment, playing a game of chess together since they had once again lost their TV, video games, computer games, iPod, iPad, Kindle, Nook, laptop, PS3, and phone privileges. Every now and then Anthony would yell that she was reading his mind and call out my name, in which I would shout back for Tammy to quit reading her brother's mind.

Normal stuff.

Now, as I was folding laundry and watching the tail end of a new cable show called *Vampire Love Story* about, of all things, MMA fighters who happened to be vampires, a car pulled up in the cul-de-sac. I looked out the window. I didn't know the car, but I sure as hell knew the tall figure who emerged.

It was Fang.

47.

We were sitting on my porch, legs and shoulders touching.

I didn't mind touching Fang. I'd always liked Fang, and even now, I considered him one of my very best friends. What he thought about me, I didn't know. Especially not now, not with his mind closed to me.

He had asked if we could talk alone. And with both kids home, *alone* meant sitting outside.

"You're looking lovely as always, Moon Dance," he said.

"Why thank you, Fang," I said.

I couldn't say the same for him. Unsurprisingly, he looked gaunt and pale. Unhealthy, at best. It was unusual for him, as he had always appeared the picture of health and vitality. He'd always been a good-looking guy, even back when I knew him only as my bartender.

Now, I found him sickly-looking. His once-handsome face was now skull-like. His cheeks sunken. Eyes dark hollows. Skin waxy. He was, I suspected, a living corpse. No doubt he was very much in need of a feeding.

"You look, um, well," I said.

He chuckled. "Bullshit. I still haven't had my first feeding, and I've only now recovered enough to function."

I motioned to the Cadillac, where Detective Hanner sat quietly. "I assume she will provide you with your first feeding."

"You assume correctly. We're heading to her place now, and then...elsewhere."

I snapped my head around. "Where?"

"I don't know yet. But somewhere not close."

"Why?"

Fang looked down at his hands, which he was opening and closing as if he was getting used to his body all over again. Or perhaps the thing inside him was getting used to Fang's body.

I shuddered.

"She's going to teach me, Sam."

"Teach you what?"

"The one thing you were never taught, what you struggled with daily. What I did my best to help you understand." He looked at me. "She's going to teach me how to be a vampire. Her and others like her."

"What is this place?"

He shook his head. "She didn't tell me much.

But it appears to be a sort of coven of vampires."

Coven of vampires? I reached out and took his cold hand. Jesus, is that what I felt like?

"She's going to teach you to kill, Fang."

He said nothing, although he did squeeze my hand back.

"She's going to teach you to kill innocent people. How to manipulate them, hurt them, take from them. She's going to teach you how to use them."

"I owe her everything, Moon Dance," he said, and now released my hand. "I owe her my life."

"No, you don't."

He moved away from me, just a few inches, but it might as well have been a few hundred feet. "She gave me the one thing that you wouldn't."

"I never denied you, Fang. I still needed to think about it. It wasn't an easy choice."

"For her, it was."

"Because she's using you, Fang. She's going to train you to be a killer. To kill for her. For them. Don't let them use you."

"They gave me everything I ever wanted—something you never would."

"But that doesn't mean you have to kill for them."

"They never said anything about killing, Moon Dance. They only want to help me, to teach me, to help me adjust."

"For what purpose, Fang?"

"I'll worry about that later, Moon Dance."

We were quiet. Sitting in the driver's seat was Detective Hanner. Her head was back. She appeared to be sleeping, but I suspected she was watching us. Indeed, every now and then I could detect a slight glow from her eyes. The flame within.

"I loved you, Moon Dance."

"Loved?" I said, wincing at the past tense.

"Yes, *loved*. But you didn't return my love. Not really. But most important, you didn't trust me. You feared me on some level. And you denied me the one thing I wanted most in this world."

"Exactly," I said. "So, how could I know if your love for me was real, or an infatuation?"

He turned his head and looked at me sharply. I saw the deep pain, but I also saw something else. Deep resentment. "You knew, Sam. You knew better than anyone how I felt about you."

And with that, he stood. He was about to walk away when he paused and, without looking at me, said, "Goodbye, Moon Dance."

He was about to leave when I reached out and grabbed his cold hand. "Wait."

He waited, still not looking at me.

I held his hand, which hung limp in my own. I debated on how much to say, what to say, and in the end, I could only say, "Goodbye, Fang."

He stood there for a second or two, then released my hand.

And left.

The End

About the Author:

J.R. Rain is an ex-private investigator who now writes full-time. He lives in a small house on a small island with his small dog, Sadie. Please visit him at www.jrrain.com.

Made in the USA
San Bernardino, CA
17 October 2017